Runaway

Runaway

NORMA CHARLES

Edited by Dave Margoshes.

Cover painting by Dawn Pearcey.
Cover and book design by Duncan Campbell.
Printed and bound in Canada.

The author gratefully acknowledges the financial assistance of the British Columbia Arts Board.

The publisher gratefully acknowledges the financial assistance of the Saskatchewan Arts Board, the Canada Council for the Arts, the Government of Canada through the Book Publishing Industry Development Program (BPIDIP), and the City of Regina Arts Commission, for its publishing program.

Canadian Cataloguing in Publication Data

Charles, Norma M.
Runaway
ISBN 1-55050-143-7

I. Title.

PS8555.H4224R85 1999 jC813'.54 C99-920023-2
PZ7.C3782Ru 1999

COTEAU BOOKS
401-2206 Dewdney Ave.
Regina, Saskatchewan
Canada S4R 1H3

AVAILABLE IN THE US FROM
General Distribution Services
85 River Rock Drive, Suite 202
Buffalo, New York, USA 14207

In memory of Sonia,
best friend and writing partner.

CONTENTS

Sent Away

"I WON'T GO!"

"You'll do as you're told, young lady."

"But-but...."

The look her father gave Toni silenced her. She clenched her teeth and flounced out of the living room.

She threw herself onto her bed. It was not fair! All her brothers got to stay home. Most of her friends got to stay home. But she was being sent away. Sent far away. At least a thousand miles away to some wretched convent on the prairies. All because *Maman* had caught her coming inside after midnight wearing her nightgown.

She wouldn't believe that Toni had just been running and dancing alone in the moonlight. She had called her a wild thing and said she was at her wits end about what to do with her very unladylike daughter.

Then Aunt Eloise, who was visiting them from

Saskatchewan, had suggested that they should send Toni to the convent in her neighbouring town of Bernardville. It was the convent that she had attended herself as a girl, as had Toni's mother. When Aunt Eloise even offered to deliver Toni personally, right to the Mother Superior there, that had clinched it.

Toni was packed up and sent away.

SHE SAT ON THE HARD SEAT in the train car and raked back her long tangled hair with her fingers. She stared out the window at the passing prairie. They had been travelling through this "nothing" sort of country all day. There was nothing to look at. No mountains or rivers or any real trees, just an odd scrubby bush now and then. Even the few towns they stopped at were not very interesting, just a few shabby houses bunched around the tall grain elevators. All there was here was sky. A huge blue sky that stretched away as far as she could see.

Aunt Eloise was sitting across from her, concentrating on her knitting. She was surrounded by balls of grey wool and strips of stuff she had already knitted. She had a broad calm face although, in the afternoon sunshine pouring through the train window, Toni could see the tired wrinkles at the corners of her eyes and mouth.

"I was hoping to finish your Uncle Ray's sweater before getting home," she said, her needles flashing. "But I won't be able to. I still have this whole arm to finish and we're almost there and...."

The train whistled loudly interrupting her. It slowed to a chugging stop.

Out the window, Toni saw they had stopped at a tiny train station. It was a dusty three-sided lean-to building where a few passengers lingered.

"Is this it?" she asked her aunt.

"No, this must be Farnsworth. But it means we'll be in Bernardville soon."

Toni swallowed nervously. The train was drawing her closer and closer to her fate.

Waiting for the train to pass was a line-up of cars on a road which crossed the train tracks. The first vehicle in the line was a strange contraption. It looked like an open car with the front hood removed and it was being pulled by a large docile horse.

"Now, will you just look at that poor family," said Aunt Eloise. "Things have been so bad for farmers around here these past few years with the drought and everything, that some people can't even afford the money to buy gas, so they convert their cars into carts their horses can pull. Can you believe that? They even have a name for them: Bennett Buggies, after our silly prime minister, William Bennett, who they say caused nothing but problems for everyone."

Toni stared at the strange vehicle. It looked as if a whole family had been crammed into the converted cart, and all their worldly possessions as well. The mother and father were in the front seat, and a gang of tattered kids were stuffed in the back surrounded by all sorts of baggage and trunks. They stared with envious eyes through the dust into the train at Toni and her aunt.

"That's probably another family pulling up stakes and moving on to try their luck somewhere else," said Toni's aunt, nodding at them. "Maybe they'll even make it across the mountains and get to the coast. Your father said they're always looking for good workers at the mill. We should tell them."

Toni shrugged.

Before her aunt had time to lower the train window and shout, "Go west, young man," the train started to move on.

As the train chugged away from the tiny station, Toni saw that it was on the edge of a small village. There couldn't be more than twenty rickety houses clustered down the sides of a dirt road. Toni certainly hoped that Bernardville would be bigger and more prosperous than Farnsworth.

She couldn't get the image of that sad family out of her mind. But why would they be envying her? At least they were together, and were not being sent off to some strange place where they didn't know one single person.

She looked around the train car. It was about half full of passengers surrounded by all sorts of baggage, baskets, wooden boxes, and bundles wrapped in blankets. Everything was covered with a fine dust from the windy prairies. Even the egg sandwich her aunt had bought for her in the dining car tasted gritty. But Toni was hungry so she munched it down anyway.

An elderly couple, a man and woman, shuffled into their car and settled with their bags into the seat across the aisle from Toni and her aunt.

Her aunt nodded at the old couple and fished around in her giant carpet bag. She drew out her wrinkled paper bag of peppermints and leaned across the aisle to offer them to the newcomers.

The old man took one and grunted his thanks. He shook out his newspaper and started to read it. Toni noticed that the paper was more than a month old. "August 8, 1934," it said on the top of the front page.

"Oh, thank you," said the woman. "Nothing like a peppermint to settle the stomach when you're travelling. Have you come far?"

"All the way from the coast," said Aunt Eloise. "Two days and two nights. I'm taking my niece here to the convent at Bernardville."

"Ah, an excellent school, they say."

"Yes." Toni's aunt shook out her knitting. "I attended the convent myself when I was a girl. Years ago, of course. And my daughter, Rose, graduated from there last year. She's at the Regina General Hospital now, studying to be a nurse."

"Is she now?" said the woman.

Toni knew that her aunt was about to tell this woman her whole boring life story, so she picked up her book and started reading.

Fury in the Plains was an exciting adventure story

about a girl named Molly, and a horse that she loved whose name was Flight, because when Molly rode him she felt as if she were flying. How Toni would love to have a horse like that! She would ride it, galloping all across those broad grassy prairies with the wind whistling past her ears, her long hair blowing free.

After a while Toni glanced out the window. Flight would be a horse like that chestnut she could see in a nearby field. The horse was a beauty who was tossing his dark brown mane at the train as it chugged past.

Toni saw something else in the field. A movement in the long pale grass. It was someone running. A little kid! A girl maybe? She saw her leap over a rock and dash to a wire fence which she scooted under on her stomach. The kid got up on the other side of the fence and stared intently over her shoulder for a moment at the train. Then she took off, and started running again, a strange limping sort of run. Toni could tell the kid was not running for the pleasure of running as she and her brother, Robert, often did. No, she was running to get away from something. Or someone.

She was running scared.

"We're almost there," Aunt Eloise told Toni. "And will I be happy to sleep in my own bed tonight! It's been almost a month I've been away. My poor aching back," she groaned, stretching out her legs. She gathered up her knitting and tucked it into her carpet bag. "Uncle Ray will be there to meet us at the station and we'll take you straight to the convent, *ma belle.* We'll get you there in plenty of time for you to clean up before supper."

Toni grimaced.

"Now don't you worry," said Aunt Eloise, looking thoughtfully at her. "You'll like it at the convent. Really you will. Those nuns will work you hard, but there will be fun times for you too. I know I certainly enjoyed my years there and your mother did as well. You'll make some good friends there. My Rose still visits with all her nice convent friends."

Toni nodded, but deep down she was still mad at her aunt. It was because of her suggestion that Toni's parents had decided to send Toni away to the convent. It was all her aunt's fault.

"They did have some strange customs, though," said Aunt Eloise, chuckling. "I wonder if the nuns still make you wear those funny bath shirts while you're taking a bath. They were so afraid you might actually see yourself with no clothes on."

The train whistle hooted loudly and its brakes squealed.

"This must be it," she said. "Finally, we've arrived at Bernardville."

Toni folded down the corner of the page to mark her place in her book. When she opened her suitcase to slip it in, she caught a whiff of her mother's talcum. It was her mother's suitcase, and, although it was full of Toni's clothes, it still smelled like her mother. No. She was not going to miss *Maman,* she told herself. She wasn't going to miss anyone one bit. She snapped the suitcase shut.

She brushed the sandwich crumbs off her navy blue trench coat and folded it neatly on her lap. There. She was ready now. As ready as she would ever be.

The Convent

THE FRONT DOOR OF THE CONVENT WAS as big and solid as a fortress door. Toni's aunt rang the bell, and the door swished opened silently. A small wizened nun enfolded in yards of black cloth appeared.

"La Mère Supérieure," said Toni's aunt.

"Ah, oui, Madame. Entrez."

Toni followed her aunt into the cavernous entry hall which smelled of floor wax and incense. She had an impression of flickering candles, dark wood, and pictures in huge heavy frames of frowning saints.

The little nun beckoned them to follow. She flitted up a broad curving staircase, her long black skirts rustling.

Toni gripped the handle of her suitcase in one hand and her coat in the other, swallowed hard, and climbed after the nun. Her aunt held onto the shiny banister and climbed too, puffing by the time they reached the second floor. They followed the nun down a long dim corridor and waited behind her while she tapped lightly on a door with a window of bumpy opaque glass. She opened the door and, with a nod, indicated that Toni and her aunt were to enter.

Toni's aunt stopped in the doorway. "Here we are then, *ma belle,*" she said, patting Toni's hair. "I must go now. We still have a long drive before we get home. Now don't you be so nervous. You'll be just fine. A big thirteen-year-old like you. We'll see you soon, maybe Thanksgiving weekend. Now, you be a good girl, and remember to watch your manners." She kissed both Toni's cheeks, then turned to follow the little nun away.

Toni took a deep breath and entered alone to face the other nun. The Mother Superior.

The nun was sitting at a polished wooden desk sorting through a folder. Toni put her suitcase down in front of the desk and waited, her leg pressed against the suitcase's cool reassuring bulk.

Outside the window, she caught a glimpse of her aunt and uncle's car driving away. It was soon out of sight, hidden by the convent's tall hedge. Now she was really alone. Totally alone. She swallowed hard and nervously squeezed her fingers under her trench coat.

She blinked the grittiness from her tired eyes and glanced around the dim office. Although very little light shone through the single tall window, the light globe hanging from the high ceiling had not been turned on. The noise from the nun's paper shuffling seemed to echo off the bare beige walls and ricochet off the green linoleum floor. The room sounded as hollow as the inside of an empty rain barrel.

It was hard to guess this nun's age. She was completely enclosed in folds of black cloth so only her face and hands were visible. From what Toni could make out in the dim light, her face seemed unwrinkled, smooth and shiny. She had thin lips and narrow eyebrows above steel-rimmed glasses. There was something stiff about the way she held her head in its snug head-covering. Her hands were also smooth. On the ring finger of her right hand was a simple gold ring, which Toni knew from her catechism studies, symbolized a nun's "wedding" to the church.

Finally the nun shut the folder and looked up at Toni.

"So Marie Antoinette Sauvé, daughter of Bibiane Alma Lacerte," she said in a stern voice, the words clipped. "Welcome to the Convent of Saint Bernadette. I was not here when your mother attended Saint Bernadette's, but if you are even half the student she is reputed to have been, I am certain that you shall fit in very well."

Toni snorted. She had been sure they'd compare her to dear *Maman.* She cleared her throat. "Toni," she told the nun. She wanted to set them all straight right from the beginning. "Everyone calls me Toni."

"At this convent, we never use nicknames. You

shall be called by your proper Christian name, Marie Antoinette."

Toni was about to protest that she hated that silly name, Marie Antoinette. It was so fancy that everyone here would think she was a stuck-up fancy-pants. But she remembered her promise to dear *Maman* to watch her manners so she bit her lip, bowed her head and muttered, "Yes, Mother Superior."

"You are two weeks late for the start of term, but no matter. I shall explain our convent rules," the nun went on in her stern, clipped voice. "You must wear your complete uniform at all times and keep it in perfect condition. You sew, of course."

This was a statement, not a question, so Toni just nodded.

"Good. Classes are from eight to four o'clock Monday to Friday and nine to one on Saturday. We expect all our girls to work hard and do their best at all times. Mass is every morning at seven o'clock in the chapel here at the convent, except Sundays when we attend High Mass at the cathedral. It is forbidden to leave the convent grounds at any time without special permission. And never, ever alone. The reputation of our convent girls is very important to us."

Toni sighed. Rules, rules. How she itched to get outside and explore. From the train she had seen that this province of Saskatchewan was a huge new country with vast skies and enormous prairie lands. So different from the green wooded mountains of the West Coast. She wanted to run and jump and see and feel it all, especially that wonderful wind. Even indoors, enclosed by thick brick walls, she was aware of the prairie wind. It hummed past the tall narrow window, rattling the panes. But those thick walls, the long dark hallways and heavy front doors made the convent feel like a fortress or a jail. What had the nun said? That they weren't even allowed out of the convent grounds without special permission? What kind of prison had her parents sent her to, anyway?

The nun went on talking, talking, talking, tapping the green blotter on her desk with her fountain pen for emphasis. Toni shifted from foot to foot in time with the tapping and the ticking of the large black clock on the bookcase behind the nun's desk. The clock's long gold pendulum swung back and forth slowly, reluctantly ticking off long seconds. Toni started to sway back and forth with it.

The nun rattled open a paper from her folder. "Now here is the letter from your mother. It appears that she has plans for you at Saint Bernadette's this year. Her wish is that you will learn to become a more genteel, responsible young lady."

Here we go, Toni thought, sighing loudly this time. She crossed her arms tightly in front of her chest. More of this "genteel young lady" stuff.

The nun glanced up, raising her thin eyebrows. "It appears you have been causing your parents a great deal of worry lately, Marie Antoinette, out running about in the woods like a wild thing, always daydreaming, not finishing your school assignments. Even missing classes! Tsk, tsk. Definitely, not proper behavior for a well bred, responsible thirteen-year-old young lady. Now, I shall tell you right off: we shall have none of that here. All our students, especially our boarders, are good hard workers. Punctuality, Neatness, and Obedience. That is our motto at Saint Bernadette's."

Toni nudged the desk leg with her toe and raked her long curly hair forward with her fingers. It fell in front of her face like a protective brown curtain. Why did *Maman* have to write all that stuff to the nun?

"I didn't want to come here anyway," she muttered, staring down at the shiny floor.

"Ah, but you are here, my dear," said Mother Superior. "And mark my words, by the end of this year, you shall not know yourself. You shall have become a proper young lady that would make your parents proud." She smiled at Toni, a tight automatic smile.

Toni glared back at the nun through her tangles.

The nun rang a small brass bell on her desk. "Sister Francesca, who is *La Directrice* in charge of all our boarders, shall conduct you to your alcove in the dormitory which shall be your home away from home for the next year. You shall have time to change into your uniform and get yourself ready for supper. And we must do something with that hair. Do you have hair ribbons to tie it back?"

"Yes, Mother Superior," said Toni, her stiff lips barely moving.

"Then see that you use them."

Soon the door was opened by a short nun with a pointy nose and sharp grey eyes. She bustled in and bowed her head to Mother Superior.

Toni lifted her suitcase and turned from Mother Superior's tight smile. She followed *La Directrice* away to the dormitory.

The Dormitory

THE NUN DIDN'T SPEAK TO TONI AS SHE followed her to the end of the long dark hall. She opened a set of double doors and nodded to Toni to enter. The dormitory was a huge room, almost as big as a gymnasium but divided into rows and rows of small alcoves. As Toni followed the nun down one long row, she noticed that the alcoves were all exactly alike. They had three wooden walls painted white, about as high as Toni could reach. A white cotton curtain which could be pulled across for privacy provided the fourth side. A narrow bed with a tight white bedspread was pushed to the right and on the left stood a white dresser with a white chair beside it. The floor was the same shiny green linoleum she had seen throughout the convent.

In a few alcoves were girls lying on their bed reading. They glanced up as Toni went past but no one said anything to her.

La Directrice stopped in front of one of the alcoves and turned back. *"Là voilà,"* she said, indicating that this alcove was to be Toni's.

A girl with a haircut like a shiny black helmet lurched out of the alcove. She was lugging a red suitcase at least twice as big as Toni's. Toni started to smile hello in a friendly way, but the girl stared at her with such narrow angry eyes that Toni swallowed back her smile.

Why is she mad at me, she wondered, as the angry girl pushed past her, hauling away her suitcase, down the row.

But *La Directrice* smiled at Toni and nodded as Toni put her suitcase on the bed and opened it. When the nun left, Toni became aware of voices. Around her, girls were talking quietly in other alcoves. While she started unloading her clothes into the dresser, the girl with helmet hair came back and joined a plump red-cheeked girl lounging on the bed in the alcove across from Toni's. She could hear the girls murmur to each other while they played cards. She couldn't understand much of what they said because they were talking in a very fast French, using lots of words Toni didn't recognize. Her three years of school French and her whole life overhearing her parents chatter at each other and some of their friends in French had not prepared her for the sort of language these girls were using.

She noticed the dark-haired girl glance over her shoulder at her and whisper something to the other girl behind her cupped hand and they both giggled. Toni overheard what sounded like, *"Platte! Oui, comme elle est platte!"* And more giggles.

"Platte?" What did that mean? Whatever they were saying, she knew they were talking about her and it was not complimentary. If she'd had any idea of befriending those two girls, their glances and silly giggling changed her mind.

That was just fine with her, she sniffed. She didn't like their looks anyway.

She tugged her curtain closed and dumped the rest of her clothes out of the suitcase. Then she snapped it shut and shoved it under the bed. Her clothes sat in a stiff lump on the white bedspread. She shook them out and stashed them into the dresser drawers and put her book under her pillow.

Then she yanked off her travelling skirt and sweater and pulled on the school uniform: a long-sleeved white shirt, a red tie, and navy tunic which *Maman* had bought for her at Eaton's uniform shop before she left on the train trip with her aunt. That was just last week. It felt as if it was months ago.

She was already wearing long black stockings and black oxfords. She tried to smooth out the wrinkles on the front of the new tunic but soon gave up. She brushed her hair with long angry strokes. The braid *Maman* had made at the back had come undone and now her curly hair was all snarly. She couldn't braid it herself so she tied it back with a dark blue ribbon. There was no mirror in her alcove to see if her hair was lopsided. But she didn't care how she looked anyway. Why should she?

She sighed heavily and lay down on the thin mattress. The pillowcase was smooth against her cheek and smelled of starch. She drew her book out from under her pillow and flipped it open but she didn't feel much like reading. She swallowed back a lonely sob and shut her eyes. At home her whole family would be gathering around the kitchen table for supper now. *Maman*, *Papa,* her two older brothers, Robert, the brother just a year younger than her, and the baby, Simon, *Maman's* special pet. Were they even thinking about her? Probably not. They probably didn't even notice her empty chair.

Her stomach grumbled. She hugged it close and waited for the supper bell to ring.

It rang soon. She wiped her face on the pillowcase and got up. She followed the other girls out of the dormitory and downstairs to the basement Refectory for supper.

It seemed as if everyone already had a special friend and had no interest in her. Besides, they were all gabbing at each other in such a fast garbled French that she understood only every second word. She felt too shy to approach anyone even after Mother Superior introduced her as coming all the way from the West Coast and saying that she was sure everyone would make her feel welcome.

She found an empty spot on a bench at one of the tables and was glad to discover that there was a rule of strict silence at all meals.

LATE THAT NIGHT Toni had to go to the bathroom so she got up and crept down the row of alcoves. All the curtains were closed and they stirred slightly as she tiptoed past them in the dark. Except for a few girls snoring lightly, all was quiet.

Beside the row of bathroom doors was a fire exit door with a square window in it and a red *"Sortie"* light glowing above it. As she opened one of the bathroom doors, a movement caught the corner of her eye. She turned and looked at the fire exit door. She gasped. It was a face in the window! A ghostly white face!

She blinked hard and looked again. Yes, there it was, staring with wild eyes into the dormitory! It must be a ghost! Her first thought was to hide. Heart pounding, she ducked into the bathroom. Then she shook her head and scoffed at herself. She knew there was no such thing as ghosts. She swallowed hard and left the bathroom to go to the window to investigate. But the face was gone. It had disappeared.

Cupping her own face, she peered out through the cold glass into the night. There was no one out there that she could see. Just the metal fire escape railings, and beyond it, a few spindly trees bending in the night wind. She took a deep breath and shook her head. It must have been her imagination. *Maman* was always telling her that her wild imagination would lead her astray one day.

Behind her she heard a movement. She whirled around! It was just *La Directrice*. She wasn't wearing the black veil that usually covered her head. Just a white, bonnet-like headdress which covered her hair. Her dark grey eyes were concerned. She folded her hands into the arms of her white nightdress and said, *"Ah, Marie Antoinette. C'est toi. Tu ne peux pas dormir? Tu es malade?"* You can't sleep? You're sick?

"No. No, I'm fine," Toni mumbled. She couldn't think of any French words so late at night. She went back into the bathroom, peed, then stumbled back down the row of alcoves. She knew the nun would stand there and watch until she reached her own bed.

English Class Disaster

"NOW, GIRLS. YOUR ATTENTION please," said Sister Marie Rose rapping on her desk at the front of the classroom the next day.

Toni fought off an enormous urge to yawn. English Literature was the last class for the day and she wasn't sure if she could keep her eyes open. It was all so crushingly boring! It was even worse than the History class right after lunch which was all in French, and Toni had a tough time understanding what was going on.

They had started the day with Math, which was fine since at least it was taught in English, and they were doing an introduction to Geometry which Toni had done already in school last year so it was pretty easy. Then they had gone on to Science, which Mother Superior taught in English as well, and it was really interesting. They were studying the five senses. So far it had been Toni's favourite class.

Sister Marie Rose had been reading a long monotonous poem in what she probably thought was a dramatic voice but which had a tendency to rise into a squeak at the end of each line.

In spite of her name, Sister Marie Rose was about as far as anyone could get from being a rose, thought Toni. The nun's face peering out from her black veil was tinged a pale beige and was as wrinkly as a raisin. Sister Marie Raisin. That should be her name. Toni stifled a smile.

The nun continued to drone on in her high-pitched squeak. "Now girls. For your English assignment yesterday you were asked to memorize the first three stanzas of 'Reveille' by A.E. Housman. I shall give you ten minutes now to take a last look at it. Then you shall all write it out completely from memory, including all the correct punctuation and spelling. You shall find it on page 198 in your *Poems Worth Knowing*. Any questions?"

Toni was not the only one to groan. The other girls around her shuffled in their desks grumbling.

"Nine minutes left," said the nun.

The girls all flipped open their poetry books and set to doing some last-minute cramming. Toni slouched down in her desk, stretched out her legs and stifled another yawn. Her desk was half way down in the row closest to the tall windows.

Something outside caught her eye. It was a long V of wild geese flying way up high in the sky over the tall hedge which surrounded the front of convent. The birds would be heading south for the winter.

South, where it was warm and beautiful and everyone could live outdoors all the time. Oh, how she wished she could escape from this stuffy classroom and fly away south with those birds! She pictured herself as one of the geese, flying way up in that blue sky, gliding on her long wings, leading the rest of her flock all the way across the dry prairies to the warm swamps and beaches in the south.

"The new girl, um, Marie Antoinette," the nun's voice squeaked, jolting Toni back to the classroom. "You know the poem so well already that you don't have to practise it?"

"No, no, not yet, Sister," Toni muttered and stared down at her book.

She heard the girl in the seat directly in front of her snicker. Toni thought the girl's name was Janeen, or something. Mean Janeen.

She was the same girl who had snubbed Toni the day before when the nun was showing her to her alcove in the dormitory. It seemed to her that none of the girls she'd met so far were very friendly. She remembered seeing Janeen whispering insults about Toni to another girl. Come to think of it, that girl was the plump, red-cheeked girl who sat behind Toni now.

The girl in front, Janeen, was a stuck-up sort of person who thought she was so absolutely perfect, from her shiny black patent leather shoes up to her shiny black hair which she wore draped over one eye, trying to look so sophisticated like the famous movie star, Hedy Lamarr.

Boarders like Janeen made up about half of the girls in the grade eight class. The other students were probably from the town or farms nearby and they got to go home after school every night. Lucky them, thought Toni.

She tried to focus her attention on the book in front of her. She couldn't even read this wretched poem and get any sense out of the words, much less memorize it. What did "Up the beach of darkness brims" mean? She had tried to memorize it the night before when she had been given the poetry book during study period after supper, and was told to have the poem memorized for English Literature class the next day. Memorizing a dumb poem like this one was so boring that she had found herself soon nodding off to sleep.

In the classroom she renewed her efforts for a few minutes, but the silly words blurred in front of her eyes, so she gave up and slipped her new library book out of her desk. It was a good thick novel she had borrowed from the convent library during noon hour because she had finished her other book, and she was itching to begin this one. *Jane Eyre,* it was called. She flipped it open to the first page and started reading. After the first couple of pages she was pulled right into the story. Jane Eyre, our heroine, was locked up for the whole night by a cruel woman in the scary Red Room where the woman's husband had died and his ghost still lurked about. Jane cowered on the cold floor, and Toni cowered with her.

"Time's up, girls," the teacher said, jolting Toni

back to the classroom. She pushed her novel back into her desk. Around her, the girls groaned again.

"Clear your desks of everything but your pen and ink while I pass out the paper," said Sister Marie Raisin. "Do your best. And remember, all punctuation counts."

Toni picked up her straight pen and dipped it into her inkwell. "Reveille by A.E. Housman," she scrawled across the top of her paper. At least she knew that part. Now how did that first line go? "Wake...." Toni thought and thought, but she couldn't remember any other words, so she dunked her straight pen into the ink well again and wrote her own poem. It was a poem about the geese flying across the huge expanse of land, stretching out their long graceful wings and flying and flying until they finally reached their destination. By Toni Sauvé, she ended with a flourish.

"Now that's what I call a real dandy poem," she muttered to herself.

The other girls were still hard at it so she started drawing a V of flying geese at the bottom of her paper. She kept her head lowered so her long hair would shield her work.

Finally the teacher said, "Time's up, girls. Pens down. Now pass your papers forward to the girl in front of you. Front people take your papers to the back. Open your books and correct the poems from the book with your pencil. Remember, spelling and punctuation count. Any mistake you miss will be counted against your own score."

What could Toni do? The girl behind her, plump Red Cheeks, passed her paper forward to Toni. Toni glanced at the tidy, blotch-free poem and the girl's name, Linda, at the top. She couldn't give that mean Janeen person her own messy paper. It didn't even have the right poem on it. So she left it on her desk and handed forward the paper with Linda Red Cheeks' poem on it instead.

Janeen hissed back at her, "But this is Linda's, not yours."

"So?" shrugged Toni, opening her poetry book intending to copy out the Housman poem on a fresh piece of paper.

"Sister," said Mean Janeen, waving her hand in the air. "The new girl won't give me her poem to mark. She gave me Linda's paper instead."

"What is the trouble, Marie Antoinette?" asked the teacher, bustling down the row to Toni's desk.

Toni tried to cover her poem with her hand, but it was no use. The nun could see that except for the title and the first word, her poem was completely different from the poem in the poetry book.

The nun started to read Toni's poem aloud. " 'Wake. As we climb above the earth into the blue, blue sky, Our long grey feathers are stroked by the wind, The wind, the perpetual prairie wind....' This simply will not do, Marie Antoinette!" squeaked Sister Marie Rose, her raisin face flushing purple. "You were asked to memorize Housman's 'Reveille.' Not this...this silliness!"

She crumpled Toni's poem into a ball with a fierceness that made Toni flinch. "You shall write out this whole poem correctly now. All six stanzas, three times in your very best handwriting. And no spelling or punctuation mistakes or you shall do it again. Now here is some more paper." She slapped the sheets onto Toni's desk.

The four o'clock bell rang, ending the day's classes. The girls shuffled in their seats but no one got up. They would not dare leave until the teacher had dismissed them.

"Add up the number of mistakes and pass the papers forward," she directed. "And now you may be dismissed. All of you, that is, except Marie Antoinette."

Toni kept her head down and concentrated on writing the poem while the other girls filed out of the classroom past the teacher who was back sitting at her desk checking over their papers.

At first Toni took her time copying the poem and wrote her neatest, but as she was finishing the first stanza, a small blotch of ink dripped onto the paper. She didn't have a blotter so she fished out her handkerchief and tried to soak up the extra ink. It didn't work very well. The small blotch became a large smudge and her fingers were soon well inked too.

She dipped her pen into the inkwell and went on to the second stanza trying to pick up the pace, as her former dance instructor would say. But it became a real disaster of blotches and smudges. When she reached the end of the sixth stanza, the blotches made it completely impossible to read. She turned the paper over and took a deep breath.

"Neat, neater, neatest," she muttered between clenched teeth. This time her pen would not cooperate. The harder she tried, the sloppier her writing became. Soon, not only her fingers were inky blotches, but the ink had smeared up her hands as well. She rubbed them down the sides of her tunic. Good thing it was dark blue.

At the front of the classroom, the teacher cleared her throat. "And now, Marie Antoinette, are we almost finished?"

"Not quite, Sister," muttered Toni. She was on her third try now. And this one was even worse.

The nun went back to her marking. The four thirty bell rang. "I must go now," she said. "Surely you must be finished."

Toni shook her head. The nun packed up her papers and swished down the aisle toward her. "Let's see how far we have progressed."

Toni tried to hide her inky scribbles with her arm. Her face grew hot with embarrassment.

"Eh, mon Dieu! Will you look at those fingers! And those hands!" squeaked the nun when she saw Toni's mess. "What ever have you been doing?"

Toni shook her head shamefully.

"It shall certainly be a bath night for you tonight, *ma fille,"* tut-tutted the nun. "And until you are mature enough to handle the pen and ink properly you shall use a pencil in English Literature Studies. Whatever did they teach you at that school on the coast?"

The Bath Shirt

OF ALL THE STRANGE CUSTOMS AT THE Convent of Saint Bernadette so far, Toni thought the bathing customs were the strangest.

Apparently Sister Marie Raisin had talked to *La Directrice*, because when it was bed time, the nun reminded the girls that it would be Toni's turn for a bath first that night, as well as little Elsie's and another girl's whose name was Elizabeth.

"N'oubliez pas vos chemises," La Directrice told the girls not to forget their bath shirts. At least Toni understood that part.

The nun went on explaining how to bathe as if the girls had never taken a bath in their lives before. It was embarrassing.

"Et les cheveux...." While the nun explained something about washing your hair, Toni's attention wandered.

It was bad enough that they were allowed only one

bath a week, since there were almost seventy boarders and only three bathtubs in the three separate bathrooms. But to be expected to bathe while wearing a silly bath shirt, that was the craziest notion of all. Since her aunt had warned her about it, Toni knew what to expect.

The bath shirt was a loose short-sleeved shirt of coarsely woven white cotton and the girls had to wear it so they would not prance about indecently naked in the bathroom even though they would be completely alone in the room and no one could possibly see them.

The bathroom was a tiny windowless room, just big enough for the tub and a high-backed chair. There was no lock, so Toni pushed the chair in front of the door. Then she turned on the water, which gushed out of the faucet in a billowing cloud of steam. It had a strange odour. Sort of sulphury, but it looked clear enough in the tub.

She shucked off all her clothes. Then she dropped the ridiculous bath shirt into the tub and stepped in after it. When the tub was about half full, she stretched out on her back in the lovely hot water, using the soaked shirt as a pillow, and turned off the faucet with her toes. She could lie flat out, this tub was so enormous. The water gurgled around her neck and into her ears and she felt her hair fanning out around her head.

She glanced down at her chest and noticed with interest that her bosoms hadn't grown any since the last time she'd had a bath, which seemed ages ago, that last night before leaving home.

At home she could have a bath any time she felt like it, although her two older brothers sometimes complained when she stayed too long in the tub. Especially her oldest brother, Joseph. He liked to spend hours in front of the bathroom mirror trying out different hair styles. She grinned when she thought of his latest. A shiny, Brylcreem look.

"Brylcreem. You look so debonair," she sang the radio advertisement.

Then she sighed. She missed her family. Even *Maman*, although she was still mad at her for sending her so far away. She especially missed Robert, who was a year younger than her and her very best friend. They usually did everything together. Sometimes he even snuck outside with her in the middle of a warm summer night, to jog down to the beach and race along the sand.

The warmth of the bath water relaxed her. It buoyed her up until she was actually floating. Now this is nice, she thought. Very, very nice.

For some reason, she found herself thinking about the geese flying by the classroom window that afternoon. How they had stretched out their long wings and glided this way and that, soaring below the clouds. If she were at home, she and Robert could play out in the vacant lot next door that they were geese flying south for the winter. They would swoop around with their arms outstretched and make loud honking noises.

Toni kicked in the warm water, her knees splashing noisily, her body wallowing in the deep water.

"Marie Antoinette. Est-ce que c'est toi?" she heard *La Directrice* knock on the door, asking if Toni was there.

"Ah, oui. C'est moi."

"Alors. Dépêches-toi."

Old nag, thought Toni.

She noticed the water had a blue tinge. Good, she thought. That ink on her hands must be soaking out. She scrubbed her fingers with the bar of sharp-smelling yellow Lifebuoy soap until the ink faded to a pale blue. Strange. The water looks even bluer now.

Then she noticed something slithering under the bath shirt. A couple of long dark snaky-looking things!

She leapt out of the water and gasped, pressing her hands to her chest. Then she realized what it was. Her long black stockings! Ha! What a joke! When she had dropped in the bath shirt she must have dropped in her black woollen stockings as well.

But darn it all anyway! Now her stockings were soaked. Her only extra pair had that huge hole in one of the knees which she had promised dear *Maman* she would darn on the train, but she hadn't got around to it. Woollen stockings were uncomfortable, but she knew from experience that wet woollen stockings must be the most tortuous garment ever invented. Particularly these new thick woollen ones that *Maman* had bought her especially for the prairie winter.

She squeezed as much water out of the stockings as

she could and dropped them into a wet mound on the floor beside the tub. There was a large bucket of pale yellowish water standing there as well. She wondered what it was for.

She dried off, wrapping her wet hair in the towel. Her hair felt awful, clumpy and stiff. Must be the sulphury smelling water, she thought, pulling her flannel nightgown on over the towel turban. She slipped on her flowered silk kimono and wrapped her other clothes around her wet stockings. She gave her sticky hair a good rub. Then she left the bathroom, handing *La Directrice* her wet towel and the soaking bath shirt.

"Bonsoir, ma petite. Et bonne nuit," said the nun, wishing her good night.

"Bonsoir, ma Soeur," said Toni.

When she went past the window in the fire exit door where she had seen that ghostly face the night before, she glanced out. Nothing but the fire escape, the dark sky, and a few twinkling yellow lights from the town beyond the high hedge.

When she got to her alcove she draped the soaking stockings over the seat of her chair under her tunic and hoped that they would be dry by the morning. She was so tired that she didn't bother brushing out her stiff damp hair. She just slipped off her kimono and crawled into bed while *La Directrice* began the evening prayers. She fell asleep instantly.

Escape From The Dormitory

THE NEXT MORNING, TONI WOKE UP very early. Her head was itchy and her hair had dried into a stiff clumpy nest. It was so tangled that she couldn't rake her fingers through it. It was probably the smelly bath water. Come to think of it, maybe that pail of water beside the tub was special water for rinsing your hair. Maybe that was what *La Directrice* was explaining and she hadn't understood.

She tossed restlessly in her bed. She raised her head and listened. All was silent around her except for the other boarders' whispery breathing. Seventy other boarders were crammed into the crowded dormitory, each in her own small alcove. And this morning, all those boarders were inhaling and exhaling, using up all the fresh air.

Her alcove was in the row farthest from the windows. The worst part of sleeping in this stuffy place with its rows of alcoves was being so far from the windows. At home in her own bedroom, she had jammed her bed right smack up against the window so all night long she could inhale deeply and fill her lungs with pure, oxygen-rich air which she knew from her science lessons was so important for good health. From her own bed at home on the West Coast, she could smell the tangy sea air and hear the call of the gulls. Here, her every breath was stuffy second-hand air, air that had already been breathed by seventy other boarders. Ugh! Her nostrils narrowed and she gagged at the suffocating thought.

The red *"Sortie"* light over the exit door leading to the hallway reflected pink on the normally white alcove walls, pink on the lumpy bed cover, pink on the narrow dresser.

Today would be her second full day at the convent and she was going to show them back home that she could be as good a student as anyone. Her two older brothers had laughed and said that she probably wouldn't last out the first week. Well, she would show them. So there.

It was still much too early to get up. The wall behind her bed seemed to lighten a bit. Dawn must be arriving behind those drawn blinds. Dawn. That magic time when everything is transformed from muted shades of grey to their real colours of greens and browns and blues. Blues. The blue of that huge prairie sky. She hadn't had a chance to see dawn actually arriving on the prairies. It must be quite a sight.

Outside, dawn was pulsing with every eye blink,

drawing closer and closer. She began to move her head in rhythm with the pulsing dawn. Then her hands, fingers snapping, feet tapping. Slowly at first. Then faster. And faster.

She threw off her blankets.

Out. Out there. She had to get out there. She felt drawn out, out and away into the beckoning fields where she could run and dance and breathe in the good clean morning air. And be free.

She grabbed up her flowered silk kimono and slipped it on over her white flannel nightie. The kimono was so long that it reached the floor and covered her bare toes. *Maman* had given it to her as a going away present when Toni left for the convent. The creamy cherry blossoms on it reminded her of their cherry trees in spring at home in their backyard. She tied on the belt and slowly, quietly pulled back the curtain to her alcove. Then she paused and listened.

A girl down the row coughed, a deep chesty cough. She turned over with a swish of blankets and coughed some more. That would be red-nosed little Elsie. Toni had sat across the table from her last night at supper and she had coughed right though the entire meal. After supper on their way to the study hall Toni had heard some mean girls tease her and say she had TB. Poor kid.

Toni held her breath and slipped down the dark row of alcoves, the beacon of the *"Sortie"* light glowing over the exit door to the hallway luring her forward.

The slightest noise would waken HER, *La Directrice*. The nun's bed alcove was placed strategically beside the exit door so she could monitor all night-time roaming. If she heard Toni prowling around so early in the morning, she would probably get up and stand there with her pointy nose and her sharp grey eyes as she had that first night when Toni had gotten up to use the bathroom. She would be so kind, so concerned, but she would stop Toni in her tracks and march her straight back to bed.

So far *La Directrice* had spoken only French to the boarders. One of the other girls had told Toni that the nun was new at the convent this year, new from Quebec, and she had never learned to speak any English at all. Toni found it hard to imagine anyone could grow up in Canada in 1934 and not know how to speak English. Everyone she knew where she came from knew at least some English.

As Toni tiptoed past the nun's alcove, she heard the sound of snoring. Loud, deep, rhythmic snores that vibrated and echoed around the dorm. Wouldn't her brothers laugh if they could hear such a dignified woman snoring so lustily? Toni grinned to herself as she reached the exit door.

She turned the handle gently, but the door clicked loudly. The nun's snoring stopped! Toni's hand froze on the door handle.

"Don't wake up!" she silently willed the nun.

The nun stirred and turned over, muttering. Then she was quiet.

She's awake! thought Toni, her heart pounding.

La Directrice is listening! Toni stood there paralyzed, her hand frozen to the door handle.

After a long while, the nun sniffled. Then she began to snore again. Loud deep snores. Toni silently, so silently, turned the door handle and eased out into the corridor.

Quickly, quietly as a dust mote, her bare feet skimming the polished floor, she flitted down the long dim hallway which was lit only by the early dawn sky glowing in the tall windows at both ends. She was about to push open the stairs door when she glimpsed a tall shadow drifting along the side corridor toward her. She recognized the stiff shoulders immediately. Mother Superior!

Toni pressed her back flat against the door and, clutching her kimono tightly around her neck, she waited in the shadowy doorway. What explanation could she possibly have for leaving the dorm at such an hour? Would the nun believe she was sleep walking? How did a person look when they were sleep walking? Were their eyes open or closed? She caught her breath and pressed harder against the door. She shut her eyes and pretended to be asleep.

She heard the nun glide closer in shiny black nun shoes, the hem of her long black skirt swishing as it swept the floor. She was humming softly and fingering her rosary beads. Toni peeked out behind her lashes and saw that the nun was staring off into the space somewhere above her head, a worried frown between those thin eyebrows. Then she swished past.

She hadn't noticed her! Toni remained riveted

against the door until the nun had swept away down the hall. Then she let her breath out in a whoosh.

Now all was silent. One, two, three.... She forced herself to count slowly to ten. Then she pushed the door open and swooped down the flight of dimly lit stairs to the grand front entrance where candles flickered in tall glasses in front of heavy pictures of saints.

She slid open a big bolt lock. Then she turned the brass door knob and pulled the massive front door open. She stepped outside and stood at the top of the front stone stairway. A cool breeze fanned her hot cheeks. Greedily she sucked in the fresh morning air. Cool sweetness filled her lungs and flowed through her like a bubbling mountain stream.

She threw up her arms and bounded down the steps to the garden path.

"Oh dawn! Sweet and lovely dawn!" she rejoiced and danced out into its crystal freshness, her long silk kimono floating out behind her like a cloud of cherry blossom petals.

Prairie Dance

A CINDER PATH WOUND ITS WAY PAST A dusty garden of shrubs in front of the convent, then along the side of the building to the back garden. Toni avoided the sharp stones by scampering along the edge of the path where the brown scrubby grass prickled her bare toes. More rough cinders had been spread on the ground in the backyard to make a big flat play area with a drooping volleyball net. She skirted around the play area to a shoulder-high board fence. She noticed a loose board, attached only on the top. She pulled the board up, gathered her kimono tightly around herself and slipped out the narrow gap between the splintery boards.

She looked around. Now she was outside the convent grounds in forbidden territory. Her heart skipped and she grinned. Forbidden. Mother Superior had told her specifically that boarders were never allowed off the convent grounds without special permission. And certainly never alone.

She stared back over her shoulder at the convent looming over the fence. Was someone up there watching her? Had anyone noticed her escape? The long rows of tall convent windows were all firmly curtained shut. The solid yellow brick walls rose four stories to the paler beige of the overhanging roof. The building stood there silent and still, accusing her.

She ducked her head and dashed away down a dirt path. The path ran along the edge of the fields which bordered the convent back garden. She saw that with the coming daylight, the fields surrounding the convent were transforming from a dull grey to rich browns and golds. Furrows of stubble left over from the early autumn wheat harvest lined the fields. Rows and rows of stubble stretched out like long thin brown fingers until, in the distance, they merged into the misty morning sky.

These enormous prairies were a country filled with nothing. No trees, no houses, no people, no hills. Just flat fields, and above the fields a huge overturned bowl of a cloudless sky. Nothing moved. No birds. Not even a fly. Under that huge sky, Toni felt so tiny, so insignificant that she could have been no more than a speck of dust blown about by the wind.

How could something like these vast prairies be filled with nothing and still really not be empty? It didn't make sense. It was like the problem Mother Superior had presented to the class the day before during Science period: How could sound exist where there were no ears to hear it? Since sound is caused by waves vibrating upon the ear drums, the teacher had explained, if there were no ears, how could there be sound? No ears, no ear drums, no sound?

Toni couldn't stand this deep thinking any more. She shook her stiff hair and stopped jogging. She stared at the eastern sky which was growing lighter and lighter with each passing moment. Far off in the distance, where the prairie met the sky, a small speck of glowing orange appeared.

As she watched, the speck grew and grew until it formed a bright wedge. The wedge blossomed into a half circle. Then there it was. The sun! The whole round glorious sun, flooding the prairies with rich glowing colours.

Toni flung out her arms. She wanted to embrace that radiant sun, to hug its warmth, its colour, its life.

"Alive!" she sang out and started bounding down the path again. "The day's alive and now I'm free! Free! Oh what a beautiful morning! Oh what a wonderful day!"

Her feet danced and she swooped along the path toward a barn at the edge of the convent board fence.

The barn was a low building, its red paint weathered to a pale rosy grey, and the roof sloped down to a dusty tangle of weedy trees which sprouted in the dirt. The barn looked deserted and empty. It had probably been abandoned during the terrible drought on the prairies which even Toni had heard about in B.C. She remembered Aunt Eloise telling her on the train that the drought had lasted for five years now and it had made southern Saskatchewan into a big dry dust bowl with barely enough food for people, much less animals. It was terrible for business, she had moaned. No one was buying new cars anymore, so Uncle Ray's car selling business wasn't doing well. Some people couldn't even afford the gas to run their old cars, like that sad family Toni had seen from the train, who had converted their car into a buggy and had their horse pulling it.

Above the barn, a pair of long-necked geese glided by on broad outstretched wings, dark silhouettes against the yellow sky. Could they have been among the geese she had seen from the classroom window the day before?

She raked back her long hair with her fingers, and raising her arms like the birds' wings, she began to dance with her bare feet drumming on the packed brown earth in front of the barn. Slowly at first, then as the sun's rays flooded over her, warming her, she danced faster and faster, rosy puffs of dust rising from her dancing feet.

Music filled her head, flowed through her, took hold of her, transporting her, and she danced faster and faster, leaping, twirling, bounding, soaring, swooping like a bird, gliding like those geese with their broad wings outstretched, into the fields, down the furrows, her silk kimono swirling about her. Faster and faster she danced to the glorious rising sun. To the coming day. She was free! Free!

She danced, soaring away out into the field, out into the wind, leaping over the furrows, scampering down the rows, then back again to the barn. She bent and swayed and eventually slowed down. She was panting hard now, her chest heaving, the blood pounding through her body. The music in her head slowed and became silent.

All was silent around her now except for the wind and her own hard breathing. The gritty prairie wind which never stopped. It had blown all day and all night since she had arrived three days ago. She raised her head and listened to the wind rustling the long grasses, bending the bare branches by the barn. It blew her long hair into a stiff veil around her face.

Above the wind she heard another sound. Something stirred. Something inside that empty barn stirred!

The Barn

TONI SHOOK BACK HER HAIR AND PUT her hand on the barn door. Rough splintery boards. As she drew the door open, the rusty hinges creaked and sent a shiver along the back of her neck.

Holding onto the door, she stood still and stared into the barn, into its deep, musty-smelling shadows. At first all she could see was the thick dusty air which looked as solid as a plank of wood in a bright ray of morning sunlight seeping through a crack in the barn wall. She blinked and tried to stare through the dust to the littered floor. There was an old wheelbarrow, some large rusty cans and pails, a heap of muddy farm tools, rakes and shovels, piles of straw.

She pulled the door open wider so she could see better. Then she crept across the sunlit dirt floor. She was sure she heard something in here. There! In the shadows in the far corner! Something moved! Her heart leaped.

A figure scurried out of the shadows and made for the door. Toni gasped and jerked back. Then she saw the figure trip over the wheelbarrow and sprawl to the floor, groaning.

Toni's heart pounded. She darted back to the door and gripped it, ready to dash away. She pushed her tangled hair from her face and squinted back into the barn. The shaft of light from the door revealed that the figure was a person! A kid! A little kid, clutching a sort of tattered blanket about its heaving shoulders.

Who was this kid? What was it doing here? Where did it come from? Certainly not from the convent, not such a raggedy creature as that.

Toni stood there and gaped. She stepped closer. Strange pale eyes, deep-set in a thin blotchy face, stared back at her.

Toni's first thought was, the ghost! Was this the "ghost face" she had seen in the dormitory window a couple of nights ago?

The figure crouched against the wall behind the fallen wheelbarrow, blanket pulled tightly, protectively across its narrow chest.

This kid is scared, Toni thought. Very, very scared. And so dirty and smelly. She could smell it from here. And so thin. How could anyone be that thin? Stick-like wrists protruded from ragged sleeves. Jagged hair fell in clumps from the scalp and over the forehead. Lips and chin were crusted with sores. A long festering gash slashed across the cheek. Snotty runny nose. Filthy feet with mud caked between bare toes.

The kid had been crying. A wet trail of tears streamed down both cheeks.

Toni's first impulse was to race back to the convent and report to the nuns that some strange child was hiding out in the barn. But when the kid whimpered like a wounded animal and tried to cringe away into the deeper shadows, Toni went closer and knelt beside it. She put out her hand to pat it, to calm its fears.

The kid cowered away from her touch, eyes down, not looking at her now.

"It's all right," Toni murmured. She cleared her throat and spoke softly as she would to a frightened kitten. "I won't hurt you, Kiddo. Really I won't. Who are you? Where did you come from?"

The kid shook its head, not answering.

"Are you lost? How long have you been here?" Toni coaxed gently, smiling. "What's your name? You can tell me, you know. Maybe I can help you."

The kid sniffed loudly and rubbed its nose on the back of a hand already crusty with dried mucus.

"I've got a brother about your age," Toni said, using her most soothing voice. "His name's Robert and he's just a year younger than I am. He's twelve. But you're probably younger than that."

The kid shrugged but still didn't say anything.

"My name's Toni. Short for Marie Antoinette Sauvé." Toni nodded encouragingly. "But all my friends call me Toni."

"Jess," the kid's voice finally whispered.

"Jess? So are you a girl or a boy?"

"Girl."

"So Jess-girl? What's your last name? What about your family? Where do you come from? What are you doing here?"

The girl just shook her head and looked away.

"Why won't you tell me, Jess? Did you get lost or something? Or are you hiding out from someone? Is that it? Someone's after you?"

The girl stared back at her and hesitated. Then she slowly nodded but she still didn't say anything.

"And you can't tell me, right?"

The girl nodded again and stared down at the dirt floor. Her top teeth gnawed on her cracked bottom lip.

Toni picked up a sharp stick and began to draw a pattern of joining circles on the dirt floor around her bare feet and waited.

What was wrong with this girl? With all those cuts and bruises, it looked as if she'd either had some terrible accident or she had been beaten. But who would hit such a small defenseless kid? Should she run back to the convent and tell the nuns there about her? She had a feeling if she did that, the girl would just run away and hide somewhere else.

Her talking seemed to relax the girl so she decided to go on.

"You know what, Kiddo?" she said. "You're really not at all like my brother, but somehow you remind me of him. Maybe it's those pale greeny-yellow eyes of yours. Cats eyes, I tell him. But he's sure not bone-thin like you. He's big for his age, big and tough. He's almost as tall as me now. And he's a laughing sort of fellow. Know what I mean? When he's not laughing with you, he's laughing at you. He loves nothing better than teasing. Tease, tease, tease. That's what he does best. And since I'm the only girl in a family of four boys, guess who he picks on. Me! But for all his teasing, I probably like him the best of my brothers. Maybe even better than our little Simon who's the baby and *Maman's* special pet. So now, Jess-girl. Tell me all about your family."

The girl blinked her strange pale eyes at Toni and rocked herself back and forth. She seemed to be relaxing a little now, less afraid.

"Don't really got no family," she said finally. Her voice was surprisingly deep and husky for such a skinny little person. It had something in it of the grit that the prairie wind blew off the fields. "Always wanted me a brother though. Tell me some more about that Robert brother of yours."

Toni shrugged and went on talking. It felt great to be talking to someone about her family, especially her brother. "Well as long as I can remember, he's been my best friend, see. We've got the greatest place in the world to play out behind our house. That's in B.C. You heard of British Columbia?"

The girl shrugged and scratched her stomach.

"It's way west of here. Way far over the other side of the mountains. Took my aunt and me two whole days and two whole nights to get here by train. Anyways, we make tree forts out in our woods and do all kinds of really interesting things, my brother and me. My mother thinks I shouldn't be playing out there in the woods but it sure beats sitting around all day in the parlour, crocheting doilies with a bunch of old ladies. Or creeping around in that silent convent. You know what I mean?"

The girl nodded and rubbed her face with her scrap of blanket.

"I got here just a couple of days ago but I already know for a fact that I'm going to really miss my Robert," Toni told her. "Fact is, I'm already missing his crazy laugh and his fun. That's the main thing they don't have around here at the convent: some plain good old *fun*. Everyone creeps around with these big long faces, whispering away. And pray! I've never known such prayerful people. We have to say a whole decade of the rosary at night before going to sleep. I tell you I almost keel over I'm so exhausted. So how long have you been hiding out here?"

The girl shrugged her thin shoulders and looked around the barn. Then she stared out the door into the fields almost as if she was expecting someone out there to descend upon her and grab her away.

"Don't rightly know," she croaked finally. "Couple days, maybe. But I ain't never felt so bloody cold, though. Lucky to find this horse blanket in here." She pulled the ragged blanket down over her dirty bare toes and stared at the flowery silk kimono which Toni had wrapped around herself.

"You like this kimono? My mother gave it to me for a going-away present. See all the cherry blossoms on it?" Toni got up and twirled around the girl and the silk kimono swirled about her.

The girl oohed with appreciation. "Ain't never seen anything so pretty."

"That's what it's like in my back yard in the spring with all the cherry blossoms blowing around. This is really too long for me, but my mother said I'm bound to grow taller in a year out here at the convent. And more ladylike, more genteel, she may as well have added because I know that's exactly what she was thinking. That's the main reason she sent me here. To learn to be a nice polite young lady. Humph!" Toni nudged a tall milk can with her toe and it toppled over with a crash.

Another gust of wind sprayed a fine grit from the fields and Toni saw the girl trembling under her ragged wrap. The fine hairs on her stick arms were standing up away from her pale flesh. She sniffed and wiped her nose again on the back of her snotty hand.

"You know what, Jess-girl?" said Toni. "You look so skinny it's a wonder that wind doesn't just pick you up and blow you clear across the fields to Regina. Brrr. Just looking at you makes me shiver." She pulled her kimono closer around herself. "Hey, you want to come up to the convent with me? It's a lot warmer in there."

"Um," said the girl, picking at the hem of Toni's kimono with thin grimy fingers. "Think maybe they got any extra to eat up at that convent?"

"Sure. They probably do, although we never see it,"

said Toni. "I guess maybe you're awfully hungry?"

"You're darn right, I'm hungry, Miss. So hungry it feels like I got a chicken scratching at my insides." The girl licked her cracked lips. "So, um. Think maybe you could get me something to eat?"

"Well. I could ask. Sure, I bet they'd give you something."

"Think maybe you could bring it to me out here?"

"You mean you want to stay hiding out here in the barn and me bring you some food?" Toni shook her head. "No siree. That just wouldn't work. For one thing, there's just not a lot of extra food around. Those nuns watch every single thing you eat so I'd have a really tough time getting you anything. Also this barn is actually out of bounds. I shouldn't even be here now. And another thing, you could probably freeze to death out here. This place is not fit for anyone to stay in. The convent's not great, but I can tell you it sure is a lot warmer than this barn."

"You think they'd let me in? It's true it sure was mighty cold out here last night. Thought I'd freeze to bits."

"Sure, they'd have to let you in. It would only be their Christian duty to help a homeless person. Especially a kid. The nuns are actually pretty nice. Strict, but pretty nice, I guess. They've got a ton of rules, so I'll probably get into heaps of trouble when they find out I was out here alone. And in my kimono. But don't you worry. Can't be helped. I can't just leave you out here all by yourself, now, can I? I'll think up some excuse. Come on. Let's get going. It's not far. Just down that path. I'll show you the way." She turned to lead the girl back to the convent.

The girl got up and pulled her blanket tighter around her shoulders. She hesitated, staring out into the fields again as if she was trying to make up her mind about what to do. Toni saw her flinch and tremble when a cold gust of wind whipped up her tattered skirt and revealed a nasty gash caked with dried blood. The cut stretched from her bare ankle all the way up to her knee.

"Holy Toledo!" gasped Toni. "That's one nasty cut!" She gulped hard. "But those nuns'll fix it up for you really fine, I bet. Come on. Let's get going. Here. I'll even let you wear my new kimono. My nightie's really thick and warm enough."

The girl hugged Toni's kimono to her chest. "Oh, thank you," she said, her pale eyes shining. "You're darn nice. You know that, Miss. Real darn nice." She dropped the filthy blanket and wrapped herself in the kimono, its hem dragging on the dirt floor.

"So let's get going," urged Toni. "You know what? I bet they're probably having toast with strawberry jam for breakfast again this morning. That's one thing about those nuns, they sure do know how to cook."

Jess licked her lips. "Strawberry jam?"

"Yes siree," Toni said. "Nothing better than lovely warm crunchy toast and homemade strawberry jam. Yum!"

Jess swallowed hard and nodded, her mind made up. "Let's get going up to that convent."

"Just a word of advice, Jess-girl. When we meet the nuns up there, you'd better watch your language."

"My language?"

"Right. No 'darns' and that kind of stuff. All right? They're pretty fussy up there."

"All bloody right, Miss."

Confronting Mother Superior

TONI LED THE WAY ALONG THE PATH back to the convent. Jess limped after her.

"That convent place looks strong and safe enough," she muttered when Toni held the loose board up so Jess could slip through the fence and into the convent yard.

"Oh, it's safe enough, all right," Toni said, as she led her around the side of the tall yellow brick building to the broad front steps. "Sometimes I think this place is too safe. Just up these stairs now."

When Toni tugged at the heavy front door, it wouldn't open!

"Drat!" she muttered. "Someone must have bolted back the door. Now what?"

Jess looked up at her with scared eyes.

"It's all right," Toni assured her. "I'll just ring the bell. Those nuns must be up by now anyway."

She pressed the bell and waited. Hurry, she

thought. She knew that if someone didn't come and open the door soon, Jess just might run away and escape. "They'll be here in a minute," she told Jess, forcing her voice to be calm.

Finally she heard the bolt being pushed aside and the door swished open.

There stood the same short wrinkled nun who had answered the door a few days before when Toni and her aunt first came to the convent.

At her side, Toni felt Jess stiffen.

"Ah, c'est vous," said the old nun. She nodded and beckoned the girls to enter.

"Come on," Toni said. She grabbed Jess's arm and almost dragged her inside. "You don't have to be so scared, Jess. The nuns won't bite."

Jess glanced around the front entrance hall as nervously as a scared mouse. When she saw the big pictures of saints lit by the flickering candles, she stood there with her mouth open. "My, oh, my, my," she whispered, staring at them. "I ain't never seen anything so grand as those."

Toni nodded and shut the heavy front door. Then she started up the broad staircase after the little nun. Jess hesitated, glancing back at the closed door.

"Come on," hissed Toni. She came back down and tugged at Jess's sleeve. "We've got to go up these stairs."

Jess shook her head and looked as if she was thinking about escaping right back out the door.

"Up here's where we'll meet the other nuns,"

Toni told her. "And they'll give you something to eat. Something really good, I bet."

Jess reluctantly turned away from the door and followed Toni and the nun, limping up the stairs, the hem of the kimono dragging behind. When they reached the long corridor Toni turned back and she saw that Jess's pale eyes where huge.

"This hallway's so long you can barely see the end," Jess hissed. "Criky! What's that?" She grabbed Toni's arm.

Someone was walking down the corridor toward them. Toni's heart thudded when she recognized the stiff figure of Mother Superior. She gulped hard. "It's just another one of the nuns," she told Jess. "Mother Superior. She's sort of the boss of this place. It'll be all right, Jess-girl. Really, it will."

Jess clutched Toni's kimono around her tattered dress and stared with huge pale eyes at the approaching nun with her swirling skirts and veils.

The elderly nun murmured something to Mother Superior, but Toni couldn't hear what it was. Mother Superior nodded to the old nun who bowed and left Mother Superior alone with the girls.

Toni bowed her head to the nun. *"Bonjour, Mère Supérieure.* I...um...found someone...this little girl...."

The nun's stern eyebrows shot above her steel-rimmed glasses. "Come to my office at once, girls."

Toni tried to smile reassuringly at Jess. "Come on, Jess. It'll be fine. I promise. Really it will," she whispered.

They followed the nun down the long corridor, Jess dragging her bare feet on the polished floor as though she couldn't believe its smoothness.

The nun's black nun shoes squeaked softly, her skirts rustled, and the beads at her side clinked. She stopped at her office door and opened it wide, beckoning with a sharp nod for the girls to enter.

Toni gently pulled Jess inside. Here in the small room, Toni could really smell her now. What a stench! She probably hadn't bathed for weeks. Maybe even months.

The room was bright with morning sunshine pouring in through the tall window onto the large desk which was piled with neat stacks of folders and books. Mother Superior sat down on the wooden chair behind her desk and inspected the girls. Her narrow nose twitched.

"Now, Marie Antoinette. Let us hear the whole story," she said finally, looking from Toni to Jess. "How and where exactly did you find this child?"

Toni cleared her throat and tugged at the hem of her nightie to cover her dirty bare feet. "I went out this morning to-um-to get some fresh air out behind the convent, and, and found this girl out there all by herself. Her name is Jess, she said. And she's, um, lost." She glanced at Jess who shook her head at her. "No, not lost, exactly. But she needs help."

Jess nodded vigorously.

"She needs our help very badly, Mother Superior. She's cold and very hungry. Almost starving. And she's hurt too. Show Mother Superior that horrible cut on your leg, Jess. Come on. Show her."

Jess started to shake her head but at Toni's insistence, she lifted her ragged skirt and raised her cut leg for the nun to see. It was oozing an unhealthy looking pus which was trickling down her ankle.

"Eh, mon Dieu!" said the nun, clutching at the cross that was hanging from a black cord around her neck. She shook her head. "What about your family, child? Your mother and father?"

"Dead," said Jess, shrugging. "I think. At least I know my mom is. And my little sister too. They got the influenza three, four years back."

"Ah. A poor orphan," said the nun. "The first thing we shall do for you, my child, I think is a good soak in a hot soapy bath."

Toni saw Jess staring at Mother Superior for a moment as if she was trying to make up her mind whether or not she should trust her. Toni found herself nodding at Jess, trying to reassure her until she finally nodded too.

"Maybe I might have a bite to eat first, ma'am? Sure am mighty hungry," she said in her gritty voice. "I ain't had nothin' to eat since a couple days now. Not really."

"Of course, child. We shall get some porridge and milk for you from the kitchen immediately." The nun picked up a small bell on her desk and rang it. A few moments later the door opened and in bustled the same elderly nun.

While Mother Superior murmured to the nun,

Toni whispered to Jess, "After you've eaten, I bet they'll let you have a bath in one of their huge bathtubs. I had one last night. You'll love it. It's really terrific."

Jess nodded.

"Now, if you follow Sister Louise, she will take you down to the kitchen and give you some breakfast. Then she will take you up to the Infirmary and see that you are settled so we can tend to those sores of yours," Mother Superior told Jess.

Jess seemed to just realize that the elderly nun was going to take her away. She started to shake her head. "Can't Toni come too?"

"Marie Antoinette will see you later, my child," said Mother Superior gently.

"Go on, Jess," said Toni. "You have to go now. I promise I'll see you later."

Sister Louise took Jess's hand and smiled kindly at her.

Jess smiled back hesitantly. Then she squared her shoulders and nodded.

The nun bowed to Mother Superior and gently led Jess out of the room, the hem of Toni's flowered silk kimono sweeping the floor behind them.

Mother Superior put her long fingers together and turned to regard Toni with her dark eyes. "And now, Marie Antoinette. Perhaps you have an explanation for wandering around alone outside of the convent so early in the morning in your nightgown and bare feet?"

All right, Toni told herself. Here goes.

"Well, um, I woke up really early this morning and it was so hot and stuffy in the dorm that I just had to get out. I guess I'm really not used to having so many people sleeping so close by. And, and once I got to the hallway, I just wanted so much, to go outside and see how the prairies would look so early in the morning."

"So you actually went outside the convent grounds to the fields? Alone? And in your night clothes?"

"Well, um, yes, Mother Superior. I guess so," Toni stared at the floor and bit her lip.

"Do you not remember that one of the rules I told you about specifically, was that you were not to leave the convent grounds without permission?"

"But I didn't really. At least I didn't go very far. Just along the fence. And that's where I found that little girl, you see."

"Hum." The nun raised her eyebrows and looked as if she didn't believe Toni. "All our rules here in the convent are made for very good reasons. From now on you must not leave the dormitory in the night for any reason. Any reason whatsoever. Is that clear?"

"Yes, Mother Superior."

"Since you are new, and perhaps not quite used to us as yet, I shall overlook this misdemeanor this once, but you must promise never to leave the convent grounds alone and unsupervised again. And certainly never, ever in your night clothes! Or there shall be serious consequences. Is that clear?"

"Yes, Mother Superior," Toni muttered, hanging her head. Her tangled hair fell forward

"Now, would you please get yourself cleaned up and dressed properly into your uniform before the bell rings for morning Mass. And that hair! Did you not use the bucket of rain water to rinse your hair last night?"

"Bucket of rain water? Oh, that's what that was for."

"The water is very hard here in Bernardville, so you must always rinse the minerals out of your hair in the rain water we collect especially for that purpose. Give it a good brushing for now. Remember our motto here: Punctuality, Neatness and Obedience."

Morning Mass

In her alcove, Toni grabbed her brush and attacked her hair. She did her best, brushing out the knots and tangles, but it was like trying to brush out a big dry haystack. She would get dressed, then try to tie it back.

She scrambled out of her nightie and into her uniform and started to pull on her long black stockings. Ug! They were still soaked. Her skin cringed away from the clammy wetness. She couldn't stand to wear them. She stripped them off and dug out her other, lighter pair. Darn! One had that holey knee with the run down to her ankle. She pulled it on anyway and twisted the hole to the inside of her leg where it wouldn't show so much. Then she buckled up the tops with garters.

She grabbed her brush again, but before she could finish brushing her hair the chapel bell for early Mass rang. She heard the other boarders rush down the rows of alcoves, so she stamped on her oxfords and hurried to follow them out of the dormitory and along the long corridors to the chapel on other side of the convent building.

When she yanked open the chapel door and skidded in breathlessly, she realized she had forgotten her tam and she had left her hair ribbons behind as well. It would not do to enter the chapel bare-headed with her tangled hair flying all over the place. She searched her tunic pocket for her hanky. It was a good big white one. She quickly put it on over her mound of stiff curls, tucking in as much as she could, and tied it under her hair at the back of her neck.

She took a deep breath and entered the dimly lit chapel. She genuflected, bowing her head to the altar. Then she slipped into a back pew in the shadows beside another boarder, a young one. She didn't know her name yet.

The girl glanced at the big white hanky on Toni's head and giggled behind her hand.

Toni ignored her. She knelt down and stared straight ahead at the altar at the front of the chapel. On either side of the raised platform were two tall white candles which flickered in the drafty room. Toni inhaled deeply the spicy smelling incense which filled the air in a thin cloud and, closing her eyes, said a quick prayer for Jess. "Please, God. Look after her," she whispered into her folded hands.

Soon a priest, wearing a white embroidered surplice which covered his long black cassock to his knees, approached the altar to begin morning Mass. Toni took another deep breath. Then she relaxed into the familiar ritual of the service.

The nuns sang *a cappella,* unaccompanied by any organ or piano music. They responded to the priest's deep voice as he conducted the Mass in front of the altar. The nuns' beautiful clear voices poured out of the high choir loft filling the chapel past its stained-glass windows to its high ceiling with delicious harmonies so sweet they made Toni's teeth ache.

The singing began with a *Kyrie.* As the chanting music flowed into Toni and through her, she swayed from side to side. Her spirit rose and sang. She began to hum quietly along with the music and tap her fingers on the back of the pew in front of her. She bent to the music now, swaying back and forth, to and fro, her elbows pumping, keeping time. The music moved her. It moved her spirit. She danced.

Then she felt the firm pressure of a hand on her shoulder, stopping her, gently pushing her down to her knees.

"Reste tranquille, ma petite," La Directrice whispered to her from behind. *"Ici on reste tranquille."* Be still, little one. Be still.

The girl beside her giggled at her again.

Toni flushed and bowed her head. She knelt down and concentrated on being as still as one of those painted statues up there beside the altar. Saint Anne or Saint Peter. She stirred only to sit, or kneel or stand at the required time. She set her chin and tucked her elbows stiffly into her sides. Every time she had to kneel, she felt the hole in her stocking ripping and growing bigger until she could feel the cold wood on her bare knee. Soon her whole leg would be sticking right out.

It was time for communion when people went up to the front of the chapel to kneel at the communion rail to receive a small wafer of bread from the priest. Toni didn't dare go up there in front of all the nuns and boarders with that huge hole in her stocking, plus the hanky on her head. She shrank back into the shadows and shut her eyes tightly, pretending to be deep in prayer so no one would notice her.

Finally, the priest turned to the whole congregation and gave it his final blessing and the Mass was over. The girls all filed out of the chapel. Toni was one of the last to leave. *La Directrice* was standing at the chapel door. She beckoned to Toni as she was leaving.

"Les bas," she said pointing to Toni's stockings. She shook her head. *"Ça, c'est un gros trou. Avez-vous une autre paire?"*

Toni nodded. The nun was asking if she had another pair of stockings.

"Et les cheveux?" The nun eyed the hanky covering Toni's hair. She tut-tutted and shook her head.

"Oui, ma Soeur," Toni said. She turned away and stomped back to the dormitory. She yanked the hanky off her head and pulled the brush through

her stiff tangled hair to gather it all into one clump. Then she pulled the clump back and tied a ribbon around it. It wasn't exactly in the centre of the back of her head, but it would have to do for now.

Now stockings. She picked up her other pair from the floor. They were still soaking wet, but she'd have to wear them anyway. Maybe she could get away with changing just one stocking, but she noticed that although both pairs were black, they were knitted with different patterns, so they would look silly if they weren't matched.

She whipped the wet stockings around over her head, trying to dry them. Then she stripped off the holey pair and pulled the wet pair back on. Ugh! They were as sodden as ever. Could it be possible they were even wetter? Whipping had not dried them one bit. Again her skin cringed away from the cold clammy moistness but, gritting her teeth, she tugged them on anyway and buckled them up with the garters.

Before she even left the dorm she was sure the damp wool itching all the way up and down her legs would drive her crazy.

During morning classes, she had to concentrate her hardest to keep from scratching at her legs in public. Although she kept wriggling in her desk, the teachers didn't seem to notice. The only one who did notice was Janeen, who turned around and hissed, "Stop wiggling, will you!"

Toni stuck her tongue out at her and tried to concentrate on her math problems.

Classes that morning seemed longer and more boring than ever. Somehow Toni's itchy legs made her whole body itchy. Her back was itchy, her arms were itchy, her face was itchy. Even her head was itchy. It made her burst with energy. She wondered how that little girl, Jess was doing. Probably lying back in that bathtub in that lovely warm water.

Finally the bell for recess rang. Toni was one of the first girls out of the classroom. She looked around the corridor. It seemed that most of the girls were going to stay inside, strolling down the halls arm in arm, chatting. There was no one she wanted to talk to, or who wanted to talk to her, for that matter, so she decided to zip outside to the backyard playground to maybe jog around a bit.

She slipped along the long corridor. But then, instead of going outside, she changed her mind and went up to the third floor. She wondered where they were keeping Jess. Mother Superior had said they would take her to the Infirmary. Was it somewhere up here?

She whizzed down the long silent corridor of the third floor, past the study hall, past the recreation room, past the music rooms where the girls, including Toni, who took piano lessons, had to practise every day. As she was about to pass another room, one that she hadn't been in before, she noticed the door was open. Maybe this was the Infirmary? She peeked in.

It was a small white room, scrubbed clean and smelling strongly of disinfectant and starch. A single light globe hung from the high ceiling. The entrance was lined with tall white cupboards with shelves of neatly stacked supplies. There was one window in the room and on either side of the window was a bed, one with a tight white cover, and on the other, under a mound of white quilt, someone was tossing restlessly. Toni peered closer. Could this be the Infirmary and that girl lying there, be Jess? Sure looked like it. Before she could investigate closer, a nun came up behind her.

"Sh, sh. *La petite dort,"* she whispered and shooed Toni away.

So this is where they were keeping Jess. Sleep was probably the best thing for her. She had looked so exhausted and starved when Toni found her.

Toni nodded at the nun and, as she continued along the corridor, she wondered where the girl had come from, and who she was. She was certainly a mystery. Mystery! She wondered again if maybe it had been her face she had seen staring in the dormitory window that first night. She was certainly pale enough to be mistaken for a ghost. Maybe she'd have a chance to ask her later.

On the walls of the corridor were large frames. Toni peered at them. They contained photographs of graduates. She hadn't had a chance to study them yet. Her mother's picture should be up there, as would her aunt's. Her eyes swept over the pictures. The early twenties. There, in a frame labeled 1912, she saw a familiar face. A younger, slimmer version of her mother's face surrounded by a cloud of curly hair. Bibiane Lacerte, said the label. So that was *Maman* all right. She would certainly not approve of Toni galloping down the convent hallways. But did Toni care? Certainly not.

She turned her back on the picture and zipped down stairs. She finally burst outside. There wasn't a single girl out in the playground. A bit of cold wind and they all stayed inside. What sissies! She didn't care about that either. She loved the wind. She dashed around the whole convent building, stretching out her legs and inhaling deeply the fresh windy air. She could smell the wheat dust from the fields.

By the time she had jogged around the whole building, even daring to squeeze through that hole in the board fence and do a big loop out into the fields, her restlessness had calmed a little. And maybe her stockings had even dried a bit as well. Panting now, wiping the sweat from the back of her neck under her knob of hair, she sped back up to the classroom. Science class was next and she didn't want to miss a minute of that. It was her favourite subject so far, although the stern Mother Superior was their teacher. She didn't allow any silliness whatsoever.

Now, as each girl entered the classroom after recess, the nun handed her a long metal two-pronged fork and told her to stand in a circle along the front and sides of the classroom. The other girls held out their forks awkwardly in front of themselves and stared at each other mystified. But Toni knew that these instruments were tuning forks and she could see Mother Superior had planned some sort of interesting experiment about the sense of hearing for them.

Standing there in front of everyone, holding her tuning fork, Toni was really glad that she had changed out of her holey stockings.

The Strange New Boarder

Although Toni's stomach was grumbling with hunger by the time the Angelus rang at noon the next day, she was one of the last to leave the classroom. Mother Superior had asked her to help put away the science experiment equipment. They had done another experiment about sound. This one had involved bottles of red-tinted water.

When she had finished dumping out the bottles into a bucket and setting them on the back shelves, she followed the other boarders clattering down the stairs to the Refectory, which was on the bottom floor next to the kitchen. The boarders ate all their meals there around scrubbed wooden tables set for six or eight. Most of the other convent students who lived in town went home for dinner.

At noon the lighting in the Refectory was always dull because the sun didn't shine through the high narrow windows at that time of the day and there seemed to be some convent rule against turning on any overhead lights during the day. The girls were supervised by *La Directrice,* who recited grace in her high thin voice before giving the girls permission to sit down and begin their meal.

By the time Toni arrived, the other girls were already rushing around the tables, elbowing each other out of the way so they could sit with their friends. Toni couldn't see any vacant places except at the table where Mean Janeen was with a couple of other girls. Everyone else was standing behind their places chatting and waiting for *La Directrice* to begin the prayer. Toni shrugged and went to stand beside Janeen. Janeen sniffed at her and flounced away to the other side of the table to stand beside her friend, Linda. She stroked her shiny black helmet hair down over one eye and narrowed the other at Toni.

Toni felt like sticking out her tongue at her again, but she didn't.

Elsie, the girl with the bad cough, was across the table from Toni, and two other girls who looked like sisters, with long dark straight hair, stood on Toni's left.

As *La Directrice* was about to make the sign of the cross to begin grace, Mother Superior swept in, her back straight and stern as usual. A small girl scooted behind her. The girl was wearing the same uniform as the rest of the boarders with the belt of her navy tunic pulled tightly around her thin waist. Her hair looked freshly combed into two tight braids and a long straight fringe which covered her eyebrows. It was a new girl Toni had not noticed before. She was about Jess's size. Could it possibly be her? Toni blinked and looked more closely.

Mother Superior put her hand on the girl's arm. She rang the little bell on the podium. *"Mes filles,"* she began her announcement. *"J'ai quelque chose très important à vous dire."*

Toni strained to follow the French. All the nuns at the convent spoke French most of the time, since they were a French community. She sighed with relief when Mother Superior switched to English.

"A very important announcement, my girls. A reminder. As you all know, one of our very important rules here is that there is to be no wandering off the convent grounds without permission. NONE WHATSOEVER. That fence has been put around the convent backyard for a very good reason. Now, I hope this rule is very clear. To each and every one of you."

Toni's heart jolted. It seemed to her that Mother Superior was looking her way, talking directly to her. But she hadn't gone that far out of the convent yard at recess again today. Just around that huge field on the other side of the fence. Her whole being had ached for the sense of freedom she felt when she was jogging around it. What was the harm in that? She brushed off the front of her tunic and rubbed the dust off her shoes on the backs of her stockings as she felt the girls start staring at her as well. Although Mother Superior did not mention names, it seemed the girls knew exactly to whom the warning was especially directed.

"In these hard times there have been many reports of homeless people wandering around the country, and some of them may even be desperate and dangerous. We wish to remind you that you may not EVER leave the convent alone. If you must walk or play around our grounds at recess or after school during your recreation period, you may. But do so in pairs or groups. We are responsible here for your safety, and we will not tolerate any further disobedience. Is that clear?"

The other girls at Toni's table stared at each other with wide round eyes,

"Desperate!" hissed Mean Janeen.

"Dangerous," Linda Red Cheeks whispered back.

Mother Superior looked pointedly in their direction. They clamped their mouths shut and stared down at their place mats.

"Now another matter," Mother Superior went on. "I wish to introduce a new boarder. I am certain each and every one of you shall do your best to make her feel especially welcome. Her name is Jessica."

Jess! So that girl was Jess! But what a transformation! For a moment Toni almost didn't recognize her. She saw her peering around the room searching for an empty seat. Mean Janeen and Linda Red Cheeks had pushed over so the two of them were taking up three spots beside Elsie on the bench across the table from Toni. They would not welcome Jess at their table.

Jess's pale eyes lit up when she spotted Toni. Toni beckoned her to come over and she slid along on the bench, pushing the two sisters to the far edge to make room for Jess. Jess nodded eagerly and limped to the place at the table beside Toni.

Toni glared straight at stuck-up Mean Janeen, daring her to make one sound of protest.

"By the way, girls," said Mother Superior. "We are not happy at the most unladylike manner with which you scrambled into the Refectory. From now until the end of this term you shall dine at the same table you have today. No more scrambling around the Refectory. That is most unbecoming behaviour for our young ladies. Remember our motto: Punctuality, Neatness and Obedience."

Oh, no! thought Toni. That meant she would have to be at Mean Janeen's table for the rest of the term! If she weren't so hungry, the thought would have given her indigestion. When she saw the sour looks Janeen and Linda exchanged, probably at the thought that they would have to share their table with her and Jess, she smirked right into their faces. Good. Anything to make those two stuck-ups uncomfortable.

IT WAS LINDA'S TURN to be the server for their table, which meant she had to get the meals from the food trolleys when they arrived from the kitchen and distribute them to the girls at her table.

When the trolleys arrived, Linda got up and, trying to smooth her short fluffy hair over one eye like Janeen's, minced away to get the food. She returned, holding her head high, peering out from behind a puff of hair with one eye and carrying a large tray with seven small bowls and a platter to their table.

She thinks she's so great, so sophisticated, thought Toni, willing her to trip over her silly feet, but she didn't. She arrived at their table safely and handed around the bowls of thick vegetable soup, starting with Janeen and ending with Jess. Then she placed the platter of homemade square biscuits and cheese slices in the centre of the table, much closer to her and Janeen's place, Toni noticed.

Before Linda had even sat down, Jess was slurping up her soup with the gusto of a starving dog. She noticed the biscuits and reached across the table to grab a handful. She dipped them into the soup and shoved them into her mouth whole as though she expected someone to descend upon her and grab the food away.

"Yum," she moaned loudly. "Mighty good grub they got round here." She was noisily scraping the bottom of her bowl before Toni had hers even half finished.

Toni put her finger to her mouth to warn Jess that talking was not allowed during meals, but Jess didn't see her. She did notice that both Linda and Janeen were staring at her with horrified eyes and they hadn't even started their soup.

"If you two ain't gonna eat up that soup, I'd be happy to gobble it up for you." Jess's loud gritty voice carried right across the silent room.

La Directrice rapped her podium. *"Ici on ne parle pas,"* the nun said severely, staring at their table.

"What'd she say?" asked Jess, pointing her thumb at the nun.

Toni put a finger to her lips again. "No talking here," she whispered.

"Ya mean you ain't allowed to talk while you eat? Well, I never heard of such a thing!"

"Hush now," Toni whispered. She ducked her head in embarrassment. All the girls were staring at them now.

Jess shut her lips up tight and nodded. She reached across the table and helped herself to the rest of the biscuits from the platter. She quickly wolfed them down, spraying crumbs over the front of her tunic, then looked around with sparkling eyes for more food. The other girls at the table continued to stare at her, their mouths hanging open, their spoons poised in mid air. They looked as if they had never seen anything like it in their entire lives. Toni grinned at Jess and finished her own soup.

It looked as if boring convent life was about to undergo a major change.

Dancing Around The Recreation Room

After school that afternoon, Toni joined the other boarders scattered around the recreation room listening to some concert music on the big wooden Victrola radio in one corner. They munched on hard oatmeal cookies and drank lemonade, which was their after-school snack.

It seemed that most of the boarders were there. The two dark-haired sisters and Elsie from her table were playing what looked like a three-handed game of Chinese checkers. The afternoon had turned cold and rainy. It was too wet for walking around the convent grounds or playing volleyball in the court behind the convent. There were probably a few girls in their alcoves in the dorm, where they could read quietly until supper time.

The recreation room wasn't a huge room compared with the study hall next door, but it was big enough for a couple of old couches and a few easy chairs as well as some card tables for board games or jigsaw puzzles.

Toni was famished. The cookies were as hard and tasteless as chunks of wood, but she found dipping them into the watery lemonade made them chewable. She leaned against a window ledge dipping and gnawing away and stared down outside at the shrubs in front of the convent. The branches trembled in the wind like scared skeletons. A cold wind for late September, Toni thought, a shiver working its way up her back. Must be colder here in Saskatchewan than at home on the coast. Her brothers would probably be out in the vacant lot having a great time playing baseball with their friends, while here she was, cooped up in this place.

The wind sent a dead leaf up to the window where it clung drenched and sodden, plastered against the glass.

Toni saw Jess perched up on another windowsill on the other side of the room, staring bleakly outside. She was alone. The other girls seemed to be avoiding her just because she was new. Toni sure knew how that felt.

She downed the rest of the lemonade and crossed the room to her. "Hey, Jess. How are you doing?"

Jess glanced up and smiled at Toni. "Hiya. Mighty glad to be in here and not out in that weather freezin' my toes off." She slurped the rest of her drink noisily.

Toni nodded. "So how did you like the bath?"

"You were darn right about it. I had such a good

long soak that even my backside came out all pink and wrinkled. Never knew anything could be so terrific. Must say I'm mighty grateful to you."

Toni shrugged and grinned at Jess's language. Now that she had been scrubbed clean, Toni could see from the light that came in the window that she had a pale freckled complexion and light reddish hair which the nuns had combed into two tight braids and long straight bangs that covered her eyebrows. Although she had been here just a couple of days, the sores around her mouth and chin seemed to be healing already and even the bruises on her neck were a fainter purple, although the long scratch which slashed across her cheek was still raw looking. Toni noticed again that her pale green eyes looked as yellow as a cat's. Just like her brother Robert's.

"So what have you been doing all day?" Toni asked her.

"Spent all afternoon downstairs with those kitchen nuns. Helping them scrub out some jars for their plum jam. That main boss lady, what's her name again?"

"Do you mean Mother Superior?"

"Right. Mother Superior. She said I could maybe start going to classes tomorrow. That'll be a treat. I ain't been to school for a long time, since I was real little."

"Really? Where were you living that you couldn't go to school?"

"Well, um..." Jess shrugged and looked away so

uncomfortably that Toni was sorry she had asked.

Someone flipped the radio station to some good country music. "Give me land, lots of land. Don't fence me in..." it blared.

"The nun's not around," Toni said. "Want to come and dance around a bit?"

"Dance? Here? You betcha!" Jess's face broke into a sudden grin, her lips stretching over her chipped front tooth.

Some other boarders were bouncing around between the tables to the lively country music of a brand new program called Don Messer's Jubilee. A couple of girls patrolled the door on the look-out for the returning nun.

Toni had found out the day before that listening to the radio was allowed, even encouraged, during recreation period as a way of keeping track of current events, as was listening to good music concerts, but "coarse" country music and dancing, especially new dances like wild jitterbugging and swing, were severely frowned upon. But whenever the supervising nun left the room, some of the more daring girls switched the radio to a modern music station and swirled around the room trying out the new dances.

Jess slipped off the window ledge and joined Toni. Toni raked the ribbons out of her hair, which still felt stiff from the hard water. She'd have to wait until next week to wash and rinse it out properly when it would be her bath night again. She shook it loose and started stepping to the music. She thought she'd like dancing with Jess. She surely wouldn't complain like the other girls did when Toni didn't follow the rigid jitterbug pattern of feet together, back, under the arm and turn around.

She closed her eyes and let the music flow into her and through her. "Don't fence me in...."

She swayed to and fro, this way and that, like the tall prairie grass in the wind. Moving her feet up and down to the beat, she let herself go and glided into the dance.

Jess followed her. Around and around the room they floated, Toni's long hair swirling about her. She twirled and swooped like the geese she had seen flying high in the sky over the prairie fields. She threw up her arms, out over her head, leaping, kicking high into the air.

"Oh my, my! Look at that acrobat!" shrieked a shrill voice that carried to Toni's ears.

"Someone thinks she's Isadora Duncan, famous cree-ative dancer," scoffed another.

"Look! She's not even wearing a slip! My, my, my!" That sounded like Mean Janeen.

Toni's face burned. Those smart-aleck girls were laughing at her. Well, she'd be happy to give them something to really gawk at.

She bent over, and flipping up the back of her tunic, she flashed her underpants at them. So there!

"Marie Antoinette Sauvé!" cried a shocked voice from the door. *"Qu'est-ce que tu fais!"*

La Directrice!

Toni gulped hard and slowly turned around. She stared up into the nun's horrified eyes.

Toni's Scraped Elbow

THE USUAL TWO HOURS OF STUDY THEY had to endure every evening after supper was extended for Toni to four long hours. She was sent straight to the study hall after *La Directrice* had lambasted her. This was one time Toni was glad that she didn't understand every word of French. But she could tell from the nun's angry tone and her purplish complexion that what she was telling her wasn't exactly complimentary. For penance, she had to have supper from a tray in solitude in the study hall, and she had to stay there until bed time. She was not even allowed to do her usual piano practice.

The only good thing about the solitary penance was that she was able to sneak in the copy of *Jane Eyre* she had started a couple of days before and now was her chance to read it as much as she wanted. She sat at a desk in the row near the windows in the study hall. She thought that she should really write a letter home but she opened the book instead, promising herself that she would write her family tomorrow.

She became so engrossed with Jane Eyre's adventures wandering around that lonely mansion and dashing through the thorny heathers in the moors that she hardly looked up after the supper hour when the other boarders filed silently into the study hall. She did notice though that Jess gave her an "I'm sorry" look before settling into the desk in front of her.

When the bell finally rang at 8:30 for the end of study period, Toni gathered up her books and was about to follow *La Directrice* and the other boarders out when one of the girls tripped over Toni's foot and sprawled out in the aisle with a grunt.

Mean Janeen. If it had been anyone other than Mean Janeen, Toni would have apologized and helped her up. But since it was that mean girl, Toni just stepped around her and followed the other girls filing out of the study hall.

In the long corridor, they could hear the sound of nuns at their evening prayer drifting from the chapel at the other end of the convent. It was a singing prayer where a single voice was followed by a chanting chorus. The tune was familiar. Was it one of Bach's studies?

As Toni followed the other girls, she hummed along quietly and started waltzing down the hall, the soles of her shoes gliding on the polished linoleum. She was Jane Eyre in her long skirts, swishing down the grand staircase in the mansion.

With her eyes closed, Toni hopped down the worn wooden stairs keeping time to the lovely music. La-lala. La-lala. La-lala, she bounced down the stairs.

Almost at the bottom she tripped over someone's foot and tumbled down the rest of the way, scraping her elbow on the wooden steps. She groaned as pain shot up her arm.

"Gol darnit, Toni! What's a matter?" Jess rushed to help her up.

Toni clamped her teeth together to stop from crying out.

La Directrice scurried back to Toni and knelt beside her, her long black skirts ballooning up around her, her eyes filled with concern. The other girls crowded around in a tight circle, gaping at Toni. Janeen was there as well, looking at her with one mocking eye, the other behind her curtain of black hair.

"Serves you right," Toni knew she was thinking. Toni bit her lower lip to try to stop the pain.

"Est-ce que c'est ton bras, Marie Antoinette?" asked *La Directrice*. Is it your arm?

"Oui," Toni whispered, rocking back and forth, cradling her throbbing elbow.

"Renee. *Vas chercher la Mère Supérieure," La Directrice* told one of the older girls.

Oh no. Not Mother Superior, thought Toni.

While *La Directrice* led the other girls away to the dormitory, Mother Superior brought Toni back upstairs to the Infirmary. Jess tagged along. Toni wished she wouldn't but she couldn't tell her to scram right in front of Mother Superior. She was embarrassed enough to meet the nun's eyes. She was sure she must have heard about the dancing and the underwear display episode in the recreation room earlier that day.

Mother Superior unlocked the Infirmary with a key which she fished out from a thick jangling key ring clipped to the waist of her full black skirt. She ushered the girls into the room where Toni had seen Jess sleeping.

"We could use a little fresh air in here," Mother Superior said as she pushed open the tall window between the two beds. "Now, Marie Antoinette. We shall have a look at this arm," she said, pointing to a wooden stool by the door for Toni to sit on.

Toni sat on the stool, holding her torn sleeve away from her scraped elbow so it wouldn't get bloody. She glanced around the room. The tall window reflected back the single light of the room, a globe suspended from the high white ceiling.

Mother Superior rummaged in one of the high cupboards through some jars and boxes of bandages.

"There now, *ma fille.* We shall wash the scrape first with some of this distilled water. There. It does not look too serious. We shall apply some of this iodine. It may sting slightly but we do not want your scrape to become infected, now do we. Would you hold up her sleeve for us, Jessica? We want to avoid a stain, if possible." The nun applied a strong smelling orange liquid with a long glass stick she had dipped into a small brown bottle.

"Ooo!" Toni sucked in her breath and gritted her teeth. Sting slightly, the nun had said? She probably loaded extra iodine onto her cut just to be mean and teach her a good lesson.

Ignoring Toni's moaning, the nun said, "We shall put on a bandage to keep it clean. Now I hope you shall be more careful going up and down the stairs in future, Marie Antoinette. You really must learn to move more sedately. You must walk gracefully, calmly, more ladylike. Watch your step. No more bouncing around like that. Set a good example for the younger girls. You will soon be a grown up young woman and you must learn to act like one. We are fortunate it was only a scrape this time."

"Yes, Mother Superior. I'll try," Toni mumbled. It was the same old story all over again. "Watch your step. Act more like a lady." That was *Maman's* old theme song.

"I understand you two are interested in dancing," Mother Superior said, raising her thin eyebrows, wrapping a white gauze bandage around Toni's elbow.

Toni swallowed hard. "Dancing?" she croaked. Her face flushed. Jess shuffled uncomfortably beside her.

"There is a time and place for everything, girls," said the nun, severely. "And a convent is certainly not the proper place for some activities."

Toni bowed her head. "Yes, Mother Superior," she mumbled.

The nun patted the bandage smooth. "Now, how does that feel, *ma fille?*"

"Much better, thank you, Mother Superior," Toni said, slipping off the stool.

The nun wiped her hands on a towel. "While we are here, I shall check how that cut on your leg is healing, Jessica."

Jess nodded and climbed up on the stool. She pulled off her stocking and the nun gently removed the bandage.

"Ooh. It looks as big and awful as before," said Toni.

"But it is coming along nicely. The redness around the cut seems to be less, so that means the infection is down already. That is one good thing. I shall apply some of this iodine again."

Jess flinched when Mother Superior applied the orange liquid to her leg, but she didn't say anything.

"Those bruises on your neck seem to be better as well," the nun said, examining Jess's neck and back. "And the scratch on your cheek is healing. Are you ready to talk about how you received such nasty injuries, my dear?"

"Like I told you it was a-a horse, ma'am. I fell offa this big old giant horse. That's all. And if I hadn't scrambled away real quick, he'd a mashed me up somethin' terrible."

"Ah," said Mother Superior nodding. "And this horse, was it at your family's farm?"

Jess shook her head and seemed to lose courage. She lowered her eyes. "I daren't tell you. Really, I daren't," she croaked.

The nun nodded and gently wrapped a fresh bandage around her leg. "You let me know when you wish to talk about it."

Jess nodded.

The nun patted the bandage smooth and helped Jess pull her stocking over it. "Tonight shall be your first night sleeping in the dormitory with the other girls. Did *La Directrice* show you where your alcove was?"

"Oh, yes, Ma'am. I'm down just a bit and across from Ton...I mean Marie Antoinette. It's rummy havin' your very own bed an' all, so clean and perfect."

"Yes, well. Now, I shall wish you girls both good night. I must go quickly now or I shall be late for evening prayers."

"Good night, Mother Superior," both girls mumbled and followed the nun out into the hall where she hurried away down the long corridor, her long black nun shoes squeaking and her long black nun skirts rustling.

Sliding Down The Banister

TONI CRADLED HER BANDAGED ELBOW and followed Jess along the hall to the flight of stairs which led down to the dormitory. Her nose was still twitching with the rusty nail smell of the iodine on her stinging elbow.

"One of them pesky girls said that Mother Superior used to be some famous scientist in Quebec. Is that true?" asked Jess.

Toni nodded. "I heard that her father was, and she used to work in his laboratory. They say that she gave it all up when she became a nun. She still teaches Science class to us."

"I told you she said I could start going to classes tomorrow. Can't wait. Think they'll allow me stay here at the convent?"

Toni nodded. "Don't see why not. For a while, anyway. Although you can't pay for the fees and stuff, can you?"

Jess stared at the floor and shook her head.

"Say, Jess," said Toni. "I'm still wondering about a whole bunch of stuff."

"What?"

"You still haven't told me anything about where you came from. And who you were running away from when you were hiding out in the barn. And how you got here. You can tell me, you know. I won't tell anyone. I'm just curious."

"I-I can't say," said Jess. "If I tell you or anyone, I'd maybe even have to go back or something. And that would be so darn god-awful."

"It must be some terrible place you came from."

"It's bloody terrible."

"Do you like it here at the convent so far?"

"Oh, yes. It's nice, darn nice. The nuns and all. It's so great having all that lovely grub. At supper time I stuffed in so blasted much I thought my belly was going to bust."

Toni nodded and grinned. "I saw you at dinner time demolishing all those biscuits."

"But some of them girls are so darn stuck-up with their noses up in the air it's a wonder they don't get terrible cricks in their necks. Though the nuns are pretty nice. Even those kitchen nuns, though they don't speak English. Still it's kind of stuffy in here. Don't you think so?"

Toni nodded. She knew exactly what Jess meant. All the nuns she had met so far, including Mother Superior, were nice enough, but cooped up in this convent building all the time with all those rules, was making her feel as if she was a caterpillar trapped in a cocoon, all bundled up with miles of strong silk thread that prevented her from stretching out and being free. Being her own true self, able to run and stretch and dance when ever and where ever she felt like it.

"How come you came here?" asked Jess. "All the way from, where d'you say? B.C.? Way over the other side of the Rocky Mountains."

"It's far away, all right," said Toni. "It's all my Aunt Eloise's fault I'm here, really. She lives not too far from this town and when she was visiting us on the coast this summer she reminded my mother about this convent. It's the school both she and *Maman* went to when they were young. Well, *Maman* grabbed at the idea of me going away to this convent for a whole year like it was a drowning man's last straw. A year with these gentle nuns would teach me to be a calm and polite and ladylike young woman. Or so she thinks. Humph!"

They were at the top of the long flight of stairs. Toni's hand was on the polished wooden banister. The hall was completely empty and quiet except for the distant murmur of the nuns at prayer in the chapel. All the other boarders would probably be in their beds in the dorm by now.

Toni stared at that inviting shiny banister, which flowed down the flight of stairs from the third floor to the halfway point, where it curved in a graceful arc before continuing all the rest of the way down to the floor below.

"You know what I've been dying to do ever since I got here?" she asked.

"What?"

"I've been dying to slide down this banister. Just look at that splendid way it curves down there, then goes all the way to the bottom. It's crying out to be slid down. I bet it'd be more fun than a roller coaster."

"Ha," snorted Jess, her pale eyes snapping. "You'd never slide down that bloody banister. I dare you to."

"I double dare you," said Toni.

"Double dares go first."

"If I go, do you promise you will too?"

Jess shrugged, then she nodded. "Sure, but I know darn well that you won't anyway."

"You want to bet?" Toni tucked up her tunic and stuck her leg over the banister, gripping it between her legs. Jess was watching her with her wide yellow eyes.

"All right. Here goes!" Toni yelled.

She took in a quick breath and pushed off. Down the banister she flew, whizzing around the curve, and skimming all the way down to the second floor where she bounced off and bounded onto the lino.

"Oh boy! That's got to be the best fun I've had since leaving home!" she hissed up to Jess. "It's your turn now."

She waited. All was quiet except for the nun's prayerful murmurs in the distant chapel. She couldn't hear Jess.

Then there was a sudden whoosh and a dark blue

streak flew by, and there was Jess tumbling off the banister into a laughing heap beside her on the floor.

Toni helped her up. Jess's face was red behind her freckles and splitting with a huge grin. "That was the best!" she breathed. "The very bloody best!"

They brushed the dust off each other's tunics. When Toni was brushing the back of Jess's skirt, she saw that there was a long rip down to the hem.

"Um, Jess." How could she tell her? "Look what's happened."

Jess felt the back of her tunic. "Holy jumping jack rats!" she cried. "A huge bloody rip! I didn't even feel it happen."

"It must have caught on this screw here," said Toni, feeling the side of the banister where it connected to the lowest support post. "Look how it sticks out."

"This is a brand new tunic and I promised them I'd take extra good care of it. Now what am I going to do? If them nuns find out I was sliding down this here banister, well, they might bloody well send me away. You don't got an extra tunic, do you, Toni?"

Toni shook her head. "This is only one I've got. Sorry."

"I just thought of something," said Jess. "There were lots of supplies up in that Infirmary. I bet I could find a needle and some thread up there. Then I could mend this rip and it'll be good as new."

"You think so?"

Jess nodded. "When I was in there I didn't spend

the whole time sleeping. I had a bit of a poke around. But the room's probably locked. The nun used one of her keys to get in, remember?"

"Right. But when she left, she was in such a rush I don't think she locked it up again. At least I don't remember her doing it."

"Good-o. I'll go up and try it. It's my only chance."

Jess started back up the stairs. Toni sighed and followed her.

"You don't have to come too, you know," said Jess.

"It's really all my fault you ripped your skirt since it was my idea to slide down the banister. Come on. We'd better hurry."

Jess shrugged and they both crept back up the stairs to the third floor. They couldn't hear nuns singing any longer. They were probably reciting their rosary now. The convent was so quiet that the girls' tiptoeing sounded as loud as a troop of giant mice scurrying about in an attic. Toni thought the nuns might be able to hear them all the way to the chapel.

She led the way down the shadowy corridor, which was lined with framed photographs of former students. She averted her eyes from the frame where she had found her mother's photograph a few days ago. It seemed to her that all the photographs were glowering down disapprovingly at them.

"Well, we have to," Toni muttered up to them

and rushed on to the Infirmary. She tried the door. It wasn't locked! It was fate, she decided as she pulled the door open. Jess followed her inside.

"Up on that shelf," Jess whispered without turning on the light. "I'm sure there's a bunch of sewing stuff up there."

Sure enough, by feeling around on the high shelf, they found a spool of dark thread and a packet of needles. Jess tucked them into her tunic pocket. She nodded at Toni and smiled her thanks. "I'll stitch it up when we get back to the dorm."

They were about to leave the room when Toni heard a swishing sound coming down the corridor. A nun must be coming! She ducked back into the room and put her finger up to her lips to warn Jess. Then she quietly clicked the door shut.

The two girls waited silently in the dark room behind the door, holding their breath.

It was two nuns, apparently, one talking to the other in a low muffled voice.

"The new girl, Jessica," It sounded like Mother Superior's voice. "The little orphan. She is a mystery. I am still unable to get any information out of her."

They were about to swish past when the footsteps stopped right in front of the Infirmary door!

Toni gasped and stared at Jess. Jess stared back, her eyes huge in her white face.

"I must check that I have locked the door," they heard the nun say. They heard the rattle of the key in the lock.

"We still don't know where she came from?" asked the other nun.

"No, and I must admit that I am quite worried about that. I must call...." Before they could hear the rest of Mother Superior's answer, the footsteps had creaked and swished away.

For a moment Toni was relieved that they had not been caught. But then, when she tried the door, the knob wouldn't turn!

"Oh no! We're locked in here!" she squealed.

Trapped In The Infirmary

"BUT, BUT DID YOU HEAR WHAT THAT nun said?" hissed Jess. "It's me she was talking about, and she said she's going to call somebody. Oh, no!"

"I'm sure it's nothing, Jess. Don't worry so much. They were just talking. Come on. Give me a hand with this door."

Jess shook her head while Toni strained to turn the knob. Then they both pushed against the door, grunting, but it wouldn't budge.

"We can't get it open. I don't believe it!" Toni said, cradling her sore elbow. She lifted her fist and was about to pound on the door. Jess caught her arm.

"Hold on there a minute, Toni. We don't want them to bloody well find us here, do we? No siree. How would we explain it? If they catch us sneaking around in here, they'd maybe send me away for sure."

Toni lowered her fist. "You're right. But it's like being a prisoner, locked in here. They can't do this to us."

"We bloody well did it to ourselves. They didn't even know we were in here. Darn it all anyway! Now what?"

Toni turned away from the door and looked around the dark room for some way they could escape without anyone knowing they had been there. The only light in the room was a dim glow coming in the tall narrow window from the night sky.

White curtains on either side of the window were billowing into the room. A fine white mist drifted ghostlike through the open window and melted into a wet puddle on the floor.

Toni went to the window and peered out at the dark night. Jess followed her.

"Will you look at that!" Toni said. "Snow! Already! And it isn't even October yet."

"Happens sometimes around here," said Jess. "An early snow, but it usually doesn't stay. Makes the farmers a mite nervous though, especially if they ain't got all their hay in yet."

They gazed out at the freezing land. It was so cold that their breath rose in a cloud above them. It was an especially windy night. The trembling trees in the convent's backyard were bent low. Wind lashed wet snow against the side of the convent and into the open window.

Toni looked sideways at the outside convent wall

and realized that she was staring out at a fire escape which had been built up to the Infirmary.

"Of course!" she said. "There's a fire escape on this side of the convent for the patients in here. We'll just zip down it and sneak back inside somehow."

"Good-o! There's a door down there I jimmied that we could use. I can show you."

"Great!" said Toni. She dashed to the fire escape door which was hidden behind the curtains. She lunged against it. It was locked as well! "This is so crazy! I can't believe they'd actually lock a fire escape door. What if there was a fire in here? That's those dumb nuns for you."

"There's got to be some way out of this darn place," muttered Jess. She pushed a chair to the window and shoved it open as wide as it would go. She pulled herself up onto the sill and leaned out so far that Toni was sure she would tumble out head first.

"Oh, be careful not to fall," she squealed, dashing over and grabbing the back of Jess's torn tunic.

"It's no use," said Jess. "The fire escape's too bloody far. I can't reach it." She kicked the wall in frustration. She bit her lip and stared outside. "Just a minute," she said, yanking at Toni's sleeve.

"Ow!" said Toni, pulling away. "That's my sore arm."

"Sorry," said Jess. "But look at that. See the stone ledge? It goes right from the window to the fire escape. I bet we could scramble along that. What do you think?"

Toni stared at the stone ledge. "You're crazy, Jess. It's way too narrow. What if we fell? It's an awful long way down to the ground. Three whole storeys!"

"I bet we could do it. Sure we could, Toni. Quit shaking your head like that. The fire escape will take us right down. I know it will."

"So it was you! That face I saw a few nights ago staring into the dorm from the fire escape was you! I thought it was a ghost!"

Jess grinned at her. "I was just looking for a place out of the cold," she said. Then she climbed out the window and crouched on the outside ledge like a small shivering monkey.

Toni grabbed hold of her tunic again and stared outside. The thick snow blowing against the convent brick wall looked almost like a veil or a net. Logically, she knew the snow would not catch them like a safety net, but it looked as if, just maybe, it would.

"Maybe you're right, Jess. Looks like no more than four or five feet to the fire escape. We should be able to manage that. Guess we have to try anyway. It's the only way out." She let go of Jess's tunic and cautiously climbed out the window too. When she crouched beside her on the ledge, the wind tore at her face with what felt like long icy fingernails. "Holy Toledo, it's freezing out here!" she gasped. She steeled herself against the cold. Then, gripping the window frame, she shakily stood up on the ledge, the fierce wind buffeting her, blowing her hair into her face. "Look. Here's a drain pipe we can hang onto," she said, grabbing a narrow pipe which ran diagonally across the space between the window and the fire escape.

"Right," said Jess. "I'll just work my way across and grab onto that bloody fire escape. Here goes."

Jess stood up cautiously on the ledge and grabbed the pipe, which was about nose level. She started moving slowly along the narrow ledge. Toni could hear her mumbling curses as she inched her way across, left foot in front of her right, one hand clutching the drain pipe and the other searching the tops of the icy bricks on the convent face for better finger holds.

"All right," she grunted back to Toni. "Almost there. Just have to grab onto that fire escape. Now!" She lunged towards the fire escape railing and fumbled. "Doggone it," she moaned. "Can't move my darn foot. It's bloody stuck!"

Toni saw that Jess's right shoe had become wedged in a narrow crack in the rock ledge. She was sprawled awkwardly against the brick face, down on one knee, her other foot stuck in the crack and her thin fingers spread out against the wall like desperate spiders.

"Hang on," Toni muttered. She grabbed the pipe and took a deep breath. Then she started inching along the narrow ledge toward Jess. When she reached her, she cautiously bent down and tried to pry Jess's foot out.

"Can't get a good grip on your foot," she grunted. "I'll have to move past you so hang on tight now. And whatever you do, don't move."

Toni prayed that the pipe above Jess's head wouldn't come loose as she placed her feet on the ledge between Jess's feet and slowly manoeuvred herself around Jess's back. She could hear Jess breathing hard, almost panting.

Finally Toni made it past her. She took a deep breath and propelled herself at the fire escape. She grabbed the icy railing with her left hand.

"Got it!" she grunted. She held onto the solid railing with all her strength, her fingers burning with the searing cold. It was like holding a solid stick of ice, a round icicle, but she forced herself to hold on tightly in spite of the throbbing in her fingers and her elbow. "Now grab my other hand, Jess, and I'll help you over here," she grunted.

Jess wouldn't even look at her now. She was staring down at the veil of snow, shaking her head.

"I can't, Toni. I can't get my darn foot out," she whimpered. "I'm stuck here. I just can't move."

"Yes you can, Jess. Don't look down. Look over here at me. See. Here's my hand. Just reach up and grab it and I'll hold on good and tight. Then you can wiggle your foot back and forth to get it out. Come on, Kiddo. You can do it. I know you can."

Jess took a ragged breath and reached up and grabbed Toni's trembling hand in a death grip. Then she slowly stood up on the ledge again and held onto the pipe with her other hand. She started working her foot back and forth. Damp snowflakes clung to her pale hair and melted on her freckled cheeks.

"Just a little more. I bet it's almost out. A little more. That's right. A little more," Toni muttered, clutching Jess's hand as hard as she ever held onto anything in her life.

Then Jess jerked forward. "It's free. My bloody foot's free!"

"Great! Good going, Kiddo!"

Toni continued to hold onto Jess's hand with all her strength as she guided her the rest of the way along the ledge, right to the fire escape. Then she grabbed Jess's shoulder, pushed her over the railing, and climbed over after her.

"There. We did it! We did it!" she said, relief flooding into her trembling legs. She rubbed her numb hands together and grinned at Jess through the falling snow.

Jess grinned back at her. "You're one crazy girl!" she laughed.

"Takes one to know one," Toni laughed back at her. "This was all your idea, remember."

They both took a couple of deep breaths and, when their knees had stopped shaking, they started down the long fire escape, the wet flakes swirling around them.

When they got to the bottom of the fire escape, they were both shivering with cold. Toni crossed her arms and hugged herself, trying to stop her teeth from chattering.

"Now what?" she said.

Jess laughed. "There's that door down here I jimmied. Remember? Come on. Follow me."

Toni followed Jess around the side of the convent to a short stairway leading down to a wide door.

"Sorry. No bloody banister to slide down here," Jess joked.

The door led into the nuns' kitchen, which was dark except for an orange glow in a big cook stove in the centre of the room. It was lovely and warm and filled with the good smells of fresh bread and apples and plum jam.

"When did you jimmy this door?" asked Toni.

"This afternoon. One of the first things I had to find out was how to escape from this place. Just in case something happens. Never know when you might need a quick getaway. Can't be too darn careful, you know."

"In case what happens?" asked Toni.

Jess didn't answer, but Toni thought she shrugged.

"The trick now will be sneaking back into the dorm without meeting any of those wandering nuns," said Toni. "And getting past L.D."

"L.D.?"

"*La Directrice.* You know, the nun in charge of us boarders?"

"So that's what you call her."

They crept down the hall and up the two flights of stairs and down another corridor to the dorm. As luck would have it, they didn't meet one single person. By the time they had snuck back into the dormitory, all the other boarders had been long in their beds and had even finished reciting their evening prayers.

As they tried to sneak past *La Directrice's* alcove by the door, Toni saw that she was sitting reading from her prayer book.

She looked up at them dozily and blinked. *"C'est très tard, mes filles,"* she said severely, getting up and coming toward them.

"Oui, ma Soeur. Nous venons de la Mère Supérieure. J'ai mal au bras," Toni held out her bandaged arm and explained that they had just come from the Mother Superior.

"Alors, allez vous couchez, tout de suite," the nun told them to go straight to bed.

"Oui, ma Soeur. Bonsoir, ma Soeur," said Toni and whisked Jess past to her own alcove. The nun probably thought they had just come back from being with Mother Superior in the Infirmary. Well, the Infirmary part was right, sort of.

Piano Practice

THAT NEXT DAY WAS BRIGHT AND SUNNY. The only evidence of the snowfall the night before was the damp ground. After classes most of the boarders went outside in the sunny back garden to play volleyball, but Toni had to do her piano practice to make up for missing last night's. Her piano teacher, *Soeur* Celeste, had organized an extra practice session for her so she could learn a Haydn *Etude* for her Royal Conservatory piano exam at the end of the month.

Jess had not been able to mend her tunic the night before because the dorm had been too dark, so she had tried to fix the rip with a couple of safety pins. *La Directrice* was very annoyed when she discovered the pins at breakfast time. For penance she had assigned Jess to do some extra mending. She was to go directly to the kitchen after school where the kitchen nuns would supervise her.

Poor kid, thought Toni. Mending really must be

the most disagreeable task imaginable. All those sharp pins and needles pricking into your fingers all the time. Here at the convent, she had heard that all the boarders had to do an hour of mending every Saturday afternoon and that would be plenty for Toni.

The piano room Toni was in was one of several small glassed-in practice rooms near the study hall. There was just enough space for the piano and a rectangular bench.

Toni started off her practice as she usually did, by doing her warm-up finger exercises. Up and down the keyboard her fingers marched. The right hand first, then the left, lifting each finger high then striking each key firmly. Then both hands together, keeping her wrists up and level, not bouncing, as *Soeur* Celeste had instructed her. All the way down to the bottom of the keyboard and all the way up to the top, slowly, each note sounding out like a stately marching step. Then faster and faster until the notes skipped and blended and ran and tripped into each other like a bunch of children playing tag at recess. There. That should be enough of that. She shook her hands. Her fingers were tingling and felt warm and loose now. She stared at the dark wood of the piano. What should she play?

Her fingers started to pick out a tune. It was "None But the Lonely Heart." She closed her eyes and played the sad chords. She felt the loneliness of the tune well up in her throat. Lonely, lonely. It was strange to feel so lonely in a place as bustling and full of people as the convent, but that was exactly how she felt sometimes: so drearily lonely. She was lonely for her own home, her own space, the wild woods out behind her house on the coast where she could run and play with her brother and their exuberant friends. Here at the convent, she was all alone. A lonely, lonely heart.

After she got her fill of the lonely tune, she opened her music book to her most favourite piece, Beethoven's *Moonlight Sonata.* Playing this piece now was like eating her dessert first. She had thought that it was the sweetest piece of music she had ever heard when *Soeur* Celeste had played it for her a couple of days ago to show her how it should sound. Toni already knew the first part by heart. She played it with her eyes closed, feeling the smooth ivory keys beneath her fingers, seeing herself dancing around under a forest of tall trees in the moonlight. She was whirling around a maple tree, her long white nightgown swirling about her. The wind hummed a hushed tune through the tree's branches.

Now clouds skidded across the dark sky, devouring the round full moon. Toni saw herself leaping across the dew-drenched garden, arms flung wide, bare legs whisking through darkened buttercups and clover.

When the clouds rolled away, the moon sent Toni's dim shadow leaping out in front of her. She danced with her shadow now, her moon shadow, twirling around the trees, under their outstretched branches, over rocks and shrubs, her skirts sweeping through long pale grasses bent to the night wind.

She danced to the moon. She danced to the wind. How she danced!

Above the lovely tune, she heard the door click open and felt a draft at the back of her neck. Must be *Soeur* Celeste checking on her that she was practising that boring Haydn *Etude* for her piano exam. She stopped playing Beethoven and ruffled her piano book open to the *Etude*. But it wasn't *Soeur* Celeste. It was Jess!

"Jess! What are you doing here? I thought you were supposed to be downstairs mending."

"I was on my way when I heard that tune. It's so pretty it made me feel all jiggly in my belly. Would you play it again?"

"I'm supposed to be practising a tricky Haydn *Etude*. If *Soeur* Celeste catches me, she sure won't be very happy."

Jess peered out the door, up and down the corridor. "No one's in sight. Just the other girls practising in the other piano rooms."

"All right, then." Toni started to play the piece again. Jess leaned against the piano and hummed softly along. Her face glowed with the music. Toni played on until she got to the end, which she finished with one last melodic chord.

"Sure wish I could play piano like that," Jess sighed. "You know this one?" She started to hum a lively modern tune which Toni recognized from the radio.

She picked out the melody. Then she added some

good strong chords with her left hand. Boogie woogie chords.

"Yes, that's it." Jess hummed along to the end. "Oh, that's so darn great! Can you teach me how to play that one?" she asked, her eyes shining.

"Here's an easy one we can play together. You just play these chords down here, like this, and I'll play the melody." Toni showed her how to play "Heart and Soul." Jess caught on quickly and soon they were both bouncing up and down on the piano bench as they made wild music together.

"Girls! What in heaven's name is going on in here!"

Toni's fingers stopped in mid air. Jess's hands crashed down on the keyboard.

It was *Soeur* Celeste. Her face was red with outrage. "That is certainly not the sort of music that is suitable for nice convent girls!" she sputtered.

Toni clasped her hands and flushed with embarrassment.

"It's all my fault, Sister," Jess started to say. "Really it is. I begged Toni to show me how to play."

"I understood that you had been sent down to the kitchen to help with the mending this afternoon, young lady."

"Yes, Sister," said Jess, lowering her head, her cheeks red.

"It looks to me as if that is where you both belong today. That'll be enough practising for you, Marie Antoinette. You will spend the rest of the afternoon with Jessica down in the kitchen helping with the mending."

Mending. How she hated mending! Toni had to concentrate hard on not groaning out loud.

"I hate mending!" she muttered to Jess on their way down to basement to the kitchen.

"So do I. But there's plenty of things that are a darn sight worse than mending, believe me."

"Like what?"

"Did you ever muck out a stinky, slimy pig sty? Now that's gotta be the most bloody disgusting work you'd ever darn well imagine."

"At least it would be outdoors."

"Right. But the stink would drive you bloody well crazy."

"So you came from a farm, did you?"

Jess shut her mouth firmly. "Can't say," she muttered.

At the top of the last long flight of stairs she stroked the inviting banister and looked back at Toni.

Toni shook her head. "No. We'd better not. That's what got us into all this trouble in the first place."

"Guess you're right," said Jess. "They sure can get a mite huffy around here." And she trudged down to the kitchen after Toni.

In The Kitchen, Mending

NOW THAT IT WAS DAYLIGHT, TONI could get a good look around the kitchen where they had snuck in the night before. It was a warm steamy room with an enormous black cook stove set in the middle of the linoleum floor. The room was filled with tempting homely smells of simmering cabbage soup and fresh baked bread.

As the girls entered the kitchen, another door beside the hallway door opened and they almost collided into one of the short kitchen nuns as she puffed in. Before the nun shut the door, Toni glimpsed a dark narrow stairway which led upwards. A strong odour drifted down which she recognized immediately. Incense. Right! The kitchen must be right below the chapel and that's where this narrow stairway must lead. That was interesting. A sort of secret passageway that led directly from the kitchen to the chapel.

The girls were shown to a low table behind the stove, beside a high window which let in the yellow light of the late afternoon sun. On the other side of the window was another door, probably leading outdoors. That must be the same door they had used the night before to sneak back into the convent, thought Toni.

The kitchen nuns were friendly enough. They obviously knew Jess already. And like *La Directrice*, they didn't speak English. Two of them lugged over an immense wicker basket with a mountain of sheets and pillowcases and towels, all of which needed mending. They pushed it onto a low table between the two girls and gave them needles and spools of thread and balls of wool. Toni was amazed there could be so many tea towels and pillowcases in the convent, much less those which needed mending. She wished she had brought along her stockings, which still had that gaping hole in the knee. If she were mending something of her own, maybe it wouldn't feel like such a waste of time.

She groaned and whispered to Jess, "I'd rather write out a million lines than do all this wretched mending."

"Ici, on ne parle pas," warned one of the nuns, shaking a finger at Toni. Here, we don't talk.

Jess opened her yellow eyes wide and wiggled her eyebrows like furry caterpillars at the nun behind her back.

It took all Toni's strength to swallow back a giggle which was bubbling dangerously up to her mouth, bursting to be let out.

After Toni had mended a pile of pillowcases with quick "come along home" stitches that made bunchy little knobs, she glared at the big basket overflowing in the middle of the table. She thought about the story of the magic pot that kept boiling more and more porridge no matter how much was taken from it. That porridge pot was like this wicker basket of clothes. No matter how many tea towels they mended, there were still more to mend.

By the end of the afternoon, when the sun had gone down past their window and the nuns had to turn on an electric light above the table, Toni had stabbed her fingers with the needle so many times that they looked like polka-dotted pin cushions. And her neck ached from looking down. She stretched her arms out over her head and sighed deeply.

Must be almost supper time, she thought, her stomach grumbling. Their usual after school snack of cookies and lemonade seemed ages ago. The nuns had baked a fresh batch of bread and some spicy raisin buns with a shiny glaze on top as well, and they were cooling on some racks right behind Toni's stool. She turned her head and tilted back until her nose was almost touching one of the trays of buns. Closing her eyes, she inhaled the delicious spicy aroma. When she opened her eyes, she saw Jess was staring at her and grinning.

Toni started to grin back, but the outside door opened and an old man with a grizzled beard shuffled in hesitantly. He was wearing an old woollen coat with gaping holes in the elbows and tied together with a string around his waist. He pulled off his battered hat and turned his rheumy eyes hopefully toward the soup pot simmering on the back of the high wood stove.

He mumbled to the short kitchen nun who was stirring it, "Please, Miss. A bit of that soup? I jus' got offa the train and I ain't et since two days ago. They said I might find a bite here."

"Qu'est-ce qu'il veut?" asked the surprised nun. She didn't understand what the man was saying.

"Il veut quelque chose à manger, something to eat," Toni told her. *"De la soupe. Il a grand faim."*

"Ah. Le pauvre monsieur!" said the little nun and scurried about to fetch the man a bowl of soup and some bread.

When the nun's back was turned, Toni saw Jess grin wider at her and sneak over to the bun rack. She scooped up a whole pan full of warm buns and stashed them inside the pillow case she had been mending. Toni didn't dare look around to see if any of the nuns had noticed. She didn't think they had. They were all interested in *"le pauvre monsieur."*

Jess motioned to her that they could sneak outside and gobble up the buns. Toni nodded. She was so hungry that she didn't think she could wait until supper. They could sneak out now! Right this minute while everyone else was staring at the old man noisily slurping up his soup at the work counter.

Toni slipped to the outside door where Jess was waiting with the warm buns wrapped in the pillowcase tucked under her arm. They were about to sneak outside when *La Directrice* came into the kitchen through the hallway door. She stood there, her grey eyes fastened on the girls.

"Marie Antoinette?" she asked, her voice tight with suspicion.

"La porte," mumbled Toni, fumbling with the door knob. *"Je ferme la porte."*

La Directrice raised her eyebrows at her and nodded. *"Je pense que c'est temps souper, mes filles,"* I think it's time for supper, she told them.

Jess shoved the warm buns wrapped in the pillowcase behind her back onto a dark shelf near the outside door and the girls followed *La Directrice* to the Refectory.

Those Irresistible Buns

ALTHOUGH TONI HAD BEEN STARVING, supper that Friday night was the most unappetizing they'd had since she first arrived at the convent. Mean Janeen was the server for their table, so she would be passing out the food to everyone at their table.

Toni was sure that she smirked down at her and Jess when she handed them the largest portions of the mushy peas, boiled potatoes and a slimy fish and onion mixture. Where had that delicious soup they had smelled in the kitchen gone, Toni wondered. Those nuns were probably keeping it for themselves.

She knew they had to finish every bit of the slimy fish before getting any dessert, and dessert that night was those delicious raisin buns with the yummy glazed topping. She choked down as much of her supper as she could by curling her tongue away from it in her mouth and swallowing hard.

Jess didn't have any trouble clearing her plate. In a couple of eye blinks her entire meal had disappeared and she was scraping her empty plate with her fork. Toni hid a huge gob of her fishy peas in her linen serviette and transferred it furtively to Jess's plate. Jess thanked her with huge eyes and soon that was gone as well.

Janeen passed around the dessert, placing a plump, delicious-looking bun on each girl's plate. When she came to Toni and Jess, she picked the smallest buns left. Toni's was so puny that she got it down in two quick mouthfuls. It was just enough to whet her appetite for more. She glared at Mean Janeen, but she just smiled back in her face. She picked up her own plump bun with its glossy sweet topping and nibbled delicately at it with her small mouse teeth.

Rat teeth, more likely, thought Toni.

LATE THAT NIGHT, TONI WOKE UP. It was so late that it must be almost morning, she thought. The bed springs creaked when she turned over and her stomach grumbled. She was so hungry her insides felt like a shriveled-up birthday balloon. She hadn't been this hungry for a long time. She couldn't get the thought of those delicious raisin buns out of her mind. She thought of the ones Jess had hidden. If the nuns hadn't noticed them, they would still be in that pillowcase on the shelf by the kitchen back door where she had tucked them. Her mouth watered. She tried to put the thought of those yummy buns out of her mind, but the more she tried, the more restless she became. That darn Housman "Reveille" poem came back to tease her. "Up, lad, up... Who'll beyond the hills away?" Away and away.

She tossed and turned for what felt like hours. Finally she threw off her blankets and rolled out of bed. She pulled on her flowery kimono, which Jess had returned when she moved into the dormitory. She would go to the bathroom for a drink of water, she thought. Maybe that would help fill her empty stomach.

She tiptoed down the row of alcoves toward the bathrooms. The dormitory was dim, the only illumination from the red *"Sortie"* light above the exit door. It made everything look rosy, the alcove walls and the closed curtains hanging in front of each alcove. She noticed that a few alcoves were empty, including Linda's, directly across from hers. Probably those girls had gone home for the weekend. Lucky them.

As she slipped past Jess's alcove, she saw her curtain was ajar. She peeked in and saw Jess was lying in her bed with her eyes wide open staring up at the ceiling.

"Hi," Toni whispered to her. "Can't you sleep either?"

Jess looked at her. "I keep thinking about those yummy buns."

"That's funny," said Toni. "That's exactly what

I was thinking about."

"I was thinking that we didn't really get our fair share from that stingy-puss, Janeen, at supper time."

"So?"

"So I happen to know where there's a bunch more."

Toni nodded. "I saw you stashing them."

"What are we waiting for?" said Jess, bounding out of bed. She shook out her long white nightgown and eased open her alcove curtains.

"You want us to get into trouble again?" whispered Toni.

"Nobody's up. They won't be getting up for a darn long time yet so there's nobody around to catch us." Jess started down the aisle between the rows of alcoves.

Toni hesitated. Then she shrugged and followed her. Their bare feet skimmed the polished floor as they crept past the alcove of *La Directrice,* who she could hear was snoring steadily. That meant the coast would be clear.

Jess grinned back at Toni, and they eased themselves out of the dormitory.

They crept down the main corridor to the staircase. This way they would avoid meeting Mother Superior in the side hall where Toni had seen her pacing back and forth a few mornings before.

They slipped down the broad drafty main staircase that led to the grand front entrance of the convent. Toni tried to avoid looking at the large heavy pictures of frowning saints which lined the dark walls all the way down to the bottom of the stairs. In the place of honour in the front hall across from the heavy front doors, hung a huge picture lit by large flickering candles in two clear glass vessels on a table in front of it. The picture was of Saint Bernadette, kneeling in prayer before a tall angel. Rays of holy light streamed from his hands to light up the saint's lovely face and her long golden hair. She was smiling as if it were the happiest moment in her life.

Jess stopped and stared up at the picture. "That's so-o beautiful," she breathed.

Toni didn't want to look at the picture of the saint and the angel. She was sure they would not approve one bit of what she and Jess were about to do. Sneaking past them on their way to steal something. But it was only fair, she reminded herself. At supper time, both she and Jess had been cheated out of their fair share of dessert.

She turned her back on the picture. "Come on," she muttered at Jess. "Let's get going." She pulled her away from the picture, and they left the grand entrance to go down one more floor to the basement.

It was a good thing they knew the way to the kitchen because the basement hallway was dark and shadowy, lit only by the dim light of the early dawn sky coming in a tall window at one end.

"Bloody creepy," whispered Jess.

Toni nodded and eased the kitchen door open.

They stood in the doorway and peered around the dim room. No one was there. It was as quiet as the rest of the convent but warmer. The only light here was from the fire glowing in the stove in the centre of the room and from the lightening sky which filtered in through the windows.

"Wonder if those buns are still there," whispered Jess, heading for the outside door. She was licking her lips and her eyes were sparkling.

"Do you think we should really take them, Jess?" said Toni, easing the kitchen door shut. She was having second thoughts now.

It was light enough to see Jess shrug. "You betcha! We're right here and no one's around to nab us. And like I said, we didn't get our fair share at supper. And you bloody well agreed. Remember?"

"Guess you're right," said Toni. "All because of that Mean Janeen."

Jess poked around the shelf by the outside door. "Yippee! They're still here!" She pulled out the pillowcase and dumped the buns onto the table. "Eight of them. That's four each."

They were as fresh and delicious as Toni had imagined. She found she was so famished she couldn't shove them into her mouth fast enough. She noticed Jess was gobbling up her share as well. It was a matter of minutes and all the buns were gone.

"Yum. Bloody delicious!" said Jess, wiping her mouth off with her nightie sleeve. She peered into the other shelves. "Think we can find something else to eat around here?"

"Don't know about you, Jess, but I'm stuffed. Maybe we should head back up to the dorm before we get caught down here. Those kitchen nuns will probably come in here any second."

That's when they heard them! Footsteps and murmuring voices in the hallway!

Toni looked at Jess and froze.

Jess stared back at her, her eyes huge in her white face. "The kitchen nuns!" she gasped.

"The secret passage!" hissed Toni. She grabbed Jess's sleeve and pulled her over to the narrow door beside the main kitchen door. She yanked it open. "I think this must lead up to the chapel."

Jess nodded and scrambled in.

As Toni silently pulled the door shut, she caught a glimpse of the main kitchen door opening.

"Boy! Was that close!" she muttered in the pitch dark.

They quietly felt their way up a steep narrow staircase. It was so dark that Toni couldn't see Jess, although she could hear her breathing right in front of her face. When they came to the top of the stairs Toni felt around for a door knob. She found it and pushed. The door opened.

It was the chapel all right. She could tell right away by the spicy incense smell. She peered out. Quiet, no movement. The only light was a candle burning steadily in a large red glass beside the altar, and a lightening dawn sky which glowed through the stained glass windows.

They crept down the side aisle toward the chapel door.

By the time Toni saw her, it was too late. Mother Superior! She was kneeling in prayer in a pew beside the chapel door.

Toni gasped. Her first impulse was to shield Jess and duck back down the stairs. But it was no use. Mother Superior had already seen them both. She rose from the pew and rushed to them, her skirts swishing and her beads clinking angrily.

"Marie Antoinette Sauvé! *Qu'est-ce que tu fais ici!*" Behind her glasses, the nun's dark eyes were blazing and her mouth was narrowed into a straight line of stern admonition. "Where on earth have you two been?"

Toni clutched her kimono shut at the neck and bowed her head. *"Bonjour, ma Soeur,"* she mumbled, her insides sinking. Were they ever in for it now! How ever was she going to explain this? She wished the ground would open up and swallow her. She wished she was anywhere but there, in front of the nun's fierce anger. She wished she was dead. She gulped hard. "We were just down those stairs, Mother Superior." She pointed to the door behind them. "Jess, I mean Jessica and me, we were downstairs in the um- kitchen." Her voice came out as small and squeaky as a tiny bird's.

"You know that you are not allowed out of the dormitory at night. And in your night clothes!" Mother Superior was so angry she seemed to have trouble controlling her voice. "We have already spoken to you about this. Have we not?"

Jess squealed behind Toni.

Toni bowed her head even lower. "Yes, Mother Superior. Sorry, Mother Superior, but we...."

She was interrupted by the morning wake-up bell.

Mother Superior raised her hand. "We do not have time to go into it now."

She marched them both straight back to the dormitory where they were met by *La Directrice* and the general bustle of girls rising and getting ready for morning Mass.

La Directrice looked surprised to see them. Mother Superior spoke to her quietly for a moment in French. Toni couldn't make out what she was saying, but she knew it was about her and Jess, and she knew that the nun was not singing their praises.

La Directrice tut-tutted and shook her head at them. Mother Superior led the girls to their alcoves. "You two are to get dressed properly for chapel and report to my office directly after Mass."

AFTER MASS, TONI AND JESS stood in front of the two nuns – short, snappy *La Directrice* and the tall and austere Mother Superior.

Toni tried to breathe deeply to calm her fluttering stomach. The four buns she had wolfed down sat in there like a big solid lump of India rubber. She folded her arms tightly over her stomach and stared at the big clock on the bookcase behind Mother Superior's desk. Its long gold pendulum swung back and forth slowly. When she glanced at Jess she saw that she was biting her bottom lip hard with her chipped tooth and blinking her pale eyes fast. Jess must be feeling even more nervous than she was.

Mother Superior's office was flooded with morning light. Since it was on the east side of the building, the sun shone directly into its single tall window first thing in the morning. Also the large light globe which was suspended from the ceiling right above their heads had been turned on. Toni was dazzled by all the bright light. It felt as if she and Jess were prisoners under a spotlight being questioned by police inquisitors.

She wiped the sweat off her forehead and tried to blink away the bright light. She narrowed her eyes and stared around the room. It was as bare as she remembered it, its walls painted the same creamy shade as the rest of the convent. Besides Mother Superior's desk and chair, the only other furniture was a narrow shelf overflowing with books and the large clock on the top shelf. Toni averted her eyes from the wooden crucifix with a dying Jesus nailed to it which was hanging above the clock.

La Directrice stood beside the desk facing the girls, her back straight, her pointy nose red, and her grey eyes reproachful. Her hands were tucked into the wide sleeves of her black robe and her snug white head-covering seemed extra tight. She bowed and nodded grimly whenever Mother Superior stopped to translate.

"I want some straight answers now," Mother Superior said, her round steel-rimmed glasses glinting angrily in their direction. "First, what were you girls doing sneaking around the convent so early in the morning?"

Toni cleared her throat. "I guess we were just feeling restless, Mother Superior."

"I cannot believe that you deliberately disobeyed me. I have already spoken to you about prowling around outside dressed in nothing but your nightgowns just because you were feeling restless. I know that your mother would be terribly disappointed with you, Marie Antoinette. As you know, she was an ideal student when she was here and she has such high expectations for you. As for you, Jessica. It appears that you are not at all a good influence here at Saint Bernadette's. Is this how you act when we have taken you in and fed and clothed you? Is this the thanks we get? It seems that you are not fitting in as well as we would expect."

"But-but we didn't go outside," exploded Jess. "We didn't go even one bloo-, one single step outside of the convent building. Truly we didn't."

Toni could hear desperation in her voice. Did she think Mother Superior was threatening to send her away?

"But whatever could you two girls have been up to?" asked the nun.

"It's all my fault, Mother Superior," said Toni,

swallowing hard. Behind her back, she squeezed one hand with the other so tightly her fingers started to throb. "Really and truly it was. It was completely all my idea and I made Jess, um, Jessica come with me. Forced her to, in fact. It was just that we both woke up so early and we were, well we were so very hungry that we just went down to the kitchen for a little snack."

"A snack!" Mother Superior picked up her black fountain pen and tapped it against the base of her telephone. Her gold ring caught the light. She stopped tapping and stared at both girls. First at Jess, then at Toni.

"Taking food that does not belong to you is outright stealing. You must know that stealing food from the kitchen, or anywhere else for that matter, is a terrible sin, especially now when so many people are going hungry. This behaviour shall certainly not be tolerated here. Surely your parents must have taught you that, Marie Antoinette."

"Yes, Mother Superior," Toni mumbled. She could her feel her cheeks flush. *Maman* would be so humiliated to hear that her daughter was a thief.

"You must understand that we are responsible for you, my dears," the nun went on. "We are responsible for all our boarders here. We cannot allow you to go wandering around anywhere in the middle of the night. Inside or outside the convent. At night, you must remain in your alcove in the dormitory where you belong and where we are able to keep an eye on you."

"Yes, Mother Superior." Toni nodded. "We understand." She would agree to anything just to finish this torturous interview.

"Oh yes, Mother Superior. You bet," said Jess, her gravely voice cracking. "I'll be so mighty good. Really I will. I won't do one single bad thing ever again. Only, please give me another chance. Let me stay here, please. Please don't send me away."

The nun looked at Jess long and hard. She didn't say anything for a moment. Then she cleared her throat and said, "During these difficult times, many strangers are wandering around the country looking for work or food. As I have told you, some of these people are very desperate, even dangerous. We must be able to trust that our girls will be where they are supposed to be at all times, but especially at night."

Toni nodded again, pushing back her long hair. "We won't do it again. I promise. Really and truly, we won't."

The nun was silent again. She tapped her fountain pen against her telephone in time with the ticking of the clock as she gazed at Toni now. She seemed to be trying to decide something. Probably their fate, thought Toni. The nun could probably read in her eyes that she was not all that sorry for taking the buns. Her only real regret was that they had been caught. She couldn't stand the nun's scrutiny any longer so she lowered her eyes and stared at the floor.

Finally the nun said, "For penance, and so that

we are able to keep a closer eye on both of you, every afternoon this week, directly after classes at four o'clock, you must report here to me for extra cleaning duties. No free time and no recreation period for either of you for one whole week. We shall start early today since Saturday's classes are over at one o'clock."

Toni tried not to grimace. Cleaning! No recreation! How mean! What an old hag! But she gritted her teeth and bowed her head humbly again. *"Oui, ma Soeur,"* she muttered.

Beside her, she heard Jess breathe such a huge sigh of relief it seemed to empty her whole body. They were not going to send her away after all. Yet.

"And now you may go. Remember, one more disobedience and you shall suffer the consequences. And they shall be severe, let me tell you. We cannot tolerate disobedient girls here at our convent. We shall be watching both of you. Very closely." She dismissed them both with a curt nod.

Toni pulled her hair back and followed Jess out into the corridor. She closed the office door with a quiet click. Jess turned back to her with a huge smile.

"Thanks, Toni, old pal, old pal. Thanks for saving my life!"

Toni wiped her sweaty palms off on the side of her tunic. "Well, it was my fault too, remember? And you must admit that those buns sure were delicious."

"Mighty bloody delicious."

Eavesdropping

"THIS CORRIDOR IS WAY TOO LONG," grunted Toni. She was on her knees applying floor wax to the already shiny linoleum on the long corridor of the second floor. "And this stupid apron is always getting in my way." Her knees got tangled in the bulky apron she had been given to protect her tunic.

Jess had an apron on as well, one even longer, so hers dragged on the floor. She had bunched it up into a long sausage around her waist.

"You're darn right," she said. "It seems like there's no bloody end to it. But it still sure beats mucking out a stinky pig sty. My tin's out of wax. Can you pass me over yours?"

Toni slid her wax tin across the corridor floor.

At first, waxing the corridor had seemed almost fun. She was waxing the right side and Jess was on the left. They made it a sort of race to see who could finish her side faster. The fun part had not lasted long though. As the Saturday afternoon wore on, the corridor grew dimmer and dimmer. The only light was from a window at the end of the hall and from one light which was suspended from the ceiling near Mother Superior's office. The other hall lights had not been turned on.

"Criky! My knees are killing me," groaned Jess, sitting back and rubbing her legs, blowing her long bangs out of her face.

"Me too," said Toni, pushing back wisps of hair that escaped their ribbons. "And my back's aching like crazy. But we better hurry. The old hag said that we had to have this whole hall waxed before supper time or no supper for us. Smells like beef stew tonight. Hope they let us have some more of those heavenly buns as well."

"I can smell it too. Bloody delicious grub they got here, you must admit." Jess began applying the wax with renewed vigor.

They had worked their way more than halfway down the corridor from the dormitory now, past the grand front entrance, almost to Mother Superior's office door.

"Pass me back the tin," said Toni. Jess slid it across to her. As Toni was dipping her rag into the wax tin and scrunching up some wax with her fingers, she heard a voice coming from Mother Superior's office.

"Sh-sh," she motioned Jess to be quiet. They stopped waxing and pressed their ears to the office door to listen.

"She is probably ten or perhaps eleven, and small for her age. Light reddish hair. Extensive bruising. Very thin. Malnourished, I would say," came Mother Superior's voice from the office.

"Sounds like she's talking on her telephone," whispered Toni.

"Right-o," said Jess, her pale eyes glowing yellow.

"As I mentioned when I called earlier, she said her name is Jess, or Jessica." Mother Superior's voice went on. "No family name."

"She's bloody well talking about me!" Jess hissed. She looked stricken.

"Fine. We shall wait for more information from you about her family or her next-of-kin," Toni heard Mother Superior's voice. "When should I expect to hear from you then? Thank you." Then she heard a clatter as the nun hung up the telephone receiver and the quick patter of her footsteps to the door.

Toni lowered her head and applied herself to waxing the floor. She didn't want Mother Superior to know she had been listening to her. Jess was also bent over scrubbing away. Her white face was hidden behind her hunched shoulder.

The office door clicked open. Mother Superior stumbled over Toni's feet.

"Oh my! I didn't notice you two here," she said, recovering her balance. She looked at Jess's white face, then back at Toni. "Have you two girls been eavesdropping?"

"Oh no, Mother Superior. We've just been waxing the floor," said Toni, shaking her head vigorously and applying the wax in quick circles on the lino.

"Hum," said Mother Superior, still looking at them. Then she nodded and strode away down the corridor, her nun shoes squeaking.

When the nun was out of sight, Jess sat back on her feet. Her face looked on the brink of tears. "Did you hear her? She said she's waiting for bloody information about my family. My bloody next-of-kin. She must have contacted the bloody Authorities!"

"She didn't say she was going to send you away or anything."

"But, but, they'll come and get me. I know darn well that they will. Maybe even *he'll* come."

"*'He?'* What *'he'* are you talking about? Have you escaped from an orphanage or something, Jess? You can tell me, you know. I won't tell anyone. I promise."

Jess looked at her, hesitating. "It's my uncle," she said finally. "I can't never go back to his blasted farm. I-I did something terrible to him. Real terrible. I-I thought maybe he was..." she faltered. "You see, he was beating the living daylights out of me and, and...."

"So those all those cuts and bruises weren't from falling off a horse like you said?"

Jess shook her head. "He don't even got a horse on his bloody farm. The nuns, they won't let the Authorities come and cart me off, will they?"

Toni didn't know what to say. What 'Authorities' was Jess talking about? Why was she so scared? What had she done? Where were her parents? Who was she and where had she really come from?

"If they do, you could always run away again," she said finally. "Right? Anyway, I don't think you should worry now. We'll figure something out."

Jess's yellow eyes were wild and her short braids stood out stiffly from the sides of her head. "Maybe I should darn well run away right now, right this very minute, while I still got a chance. Before they come and grab me." Her thin body was tense, ready to take off.

"Don't be crazy, Jess. Where could you go? Hide out in someone's barn again? You wouldn't get far. Winter's coming. It's freezing out there. It snowed just the other night, remember?"

Jess shook her head. "I just don't know what to do. I really don't want to leave this convent. The nuns are bloody nice though they do get a mite huffy now and then. And-and, I never had me a real true friend before, Toni. Never in my whole life."

"Humph," said Toni, clearing her throat. She had a prickly feeling behind her eyes that she knew had nothing to do with the smell of wax. "We'll figure out a plan so you won't have to leave, Kiddo, so don't you worry. One thing for sure. You can't leave before supper. And that's that. Just smell that heavenly stew. It must be almost supper time so we better hurry and finish this waxing job, or there'll be none of that stew for either of us."

As Toni started waxing the floor again, she heard Jess utter a heavy sigh that seemed to come up all the way from her toes. Then she started waxing as well. They slid the tin back and forth across the corridor and rubbed the wax onto the floor down to the end, finishing just as the bell rang for supper.

Heavenly Stew, For Some

THE DINING HALL SEEMED DIMMER than usual that evening. Very little daylight leaked in through the long uncurtained windows from the dark sky, and only one lamp had been turned on in the room. That was the one in the centre of the room which shed light only on those tables directly under it, so Toni and Jess's table, which was off to the side next to the wall, was almost in darkness.

The girls shuffled to their places around the tables. Standing quietly, they lowered their eyes and clasped their hands together while *La Directrice* recited the grace. As they were rustling into their seats, Toni noticed Mother Superior rush into the Refectory. Her forehead was creased by a worried frown. She bowed to whisper something to *La Directrice*. She nodded and they both glanced over at Toni and Jess's table.

"Oh no!" whispered Jess, ducking her head.

"They're bloody well coming to take me away now!" She looked ready to escape under the table.

But they were not coming to get her after all. It seemed that whatever plan they had, they were not going to do anything about it at the moment. Toni saw Mother Superior nod, then whisk out of the room.

She waited silently at her place beside Jess. Linda wasn't there, so that left six girls altogether at their table. Toni noticed that Janeen, who was sitting across from them, was watching her and Jess as though she was wondering what was going on between them. Toni looked down and studied her clasped hands. Then she looked up and saw that Jess's yellow eyes were huge with fear. She reached under the table and squeezed her arm and gave her what she hoped was an encouraging smile.

The silence of the room was broken by the sound of clinking dishes as two kitchen nuns wheeled in trolleys laden with the meals. It was Toni's turn to be the server that evening for their table. Here was her chance to show everyone how serving should be done. The proper way to do it. She would not be rude. She would not be stingy. She would not serve herself and her friend first, giving herself and her friend the largest and best servings, even if they were both famished. No. She would serve all the other girls at her table first, even if beef stew and fresh baked bread must be her favourite food, even though she had not had an afternoon snack that day because of the extra cleaning duty and she was famished.

She got a tray with five bowls filled to the brim with fragrant mouth-watering stew and a plate of thick slices of bread from one of the trolleys. Then she politely handed them around to the other girls at her table, first, to little Elsie, then to the dark-haired sisters, Betty and Bertha, then to Janeen, and finally to Jess. When she placed a thick piece of bread beside each bowl, the girls all nodded their thanks.

Toni went back to the trolley for her own bowl of stew. The kitchen nun was scraping the bottom of the big stew pot to fill the remaining bowl. Did it seem to be filled even more than the others? Oh well, it wasn't her fault. It was the last bowl. She didn't want to look greedy but what could she do? She nodded thank you to the nun and put it on her tray with six glasses of water.

She was on her way back to her table in the dim light, when she stumbled over a chair leg. She crashed to the floor. She gasped as the bowl of stew gushed down like a mud slide over the front of her tunic, along with the glasses of water which soaked through to her underwear and her stockings. Jess was at her side in a flash.

"You all right, Toni?" she whispered.

Toni felt her face blazing with embarrassment.

"'Course, I'm all right," she muttered. She untangled herself from the tray and the spilled stew and water.

"Nothing's broke, at least," said Jess, picking up the glasses and putting them on the nearest table.

One of the girls from that table came to help her.

La Directrice swept over, tut-tutting at Toni. She helped her wipe the stew off her tunic and soak up the water with a handful of linen serviettes and a large dishcloth.

When Toni was more or less cleaned up, she followed Jess back to the table. All the girls stared at Toni as she lowered herself to her place on the bench. She swallowed hard and wished that she could disappear into some deep hole. She thought she heard someone tittering. But it wasn't Janeen this time. It was coming from another table. She wasn't sure, but when she glanced up, she thought Janeen was looking at her sympathetically. Could that be true? Little Elsie surely looked sorry for her.

A kitchen nun arrived carrying a small plate with a plain bun and some thin slices of cheese. *"Je regret, il n'y a plus de ragout, ce soir,"* she whispered setting the plate in front of Toni. There wasn't any more stew tonight, so Toni would have to be satisfied with this bit of cheese instead.

Jess pushed her bowl of stew towards Toni. "I'm not all that hungry," she whispered. "Go ahead. You have it."

Toni knew that Jess must be at least as famished as she was. She shook her head, but Jess insisted. She spooned a large half of her stew onto Toni's plate and pushed it in front of her with an encouraging nod.

Janeen broke her thick slice of bread in two. "Here," she whispered, and put a generous piece beside Toni's plate.

Toni raised her eyebrows. Then she smiled and nodded her thanks. So maybe Mean Janeen wasn't completely rotten after all, she thought as she dipped the bread into her plate of stew. That first mouthful of stew tasted like ambrosia, food for the gods.

As she mopped up the last bit of gravy from her plate with the last crust of bread, she promised herself that there was no way that anyone was going to come and take Jess away. She would find a way for Jess to stay here at the convent where she would be safe from those mean "Authorities" she talked about. Whatever they were. Or mean uncles, for that matter.

THAT EVENING, WHILE THE OTHER GIRLS had a quiet free time to read or sew, Toni had to do another piano practice. She was determined this time to do the right thing and not get into any more trouble with *Soeur* Celeste. One afternoon spent in the kitchen mending was enough for her. So after she had warmed up with the finger exercises and scales, she started to practise the Haydn *Etude* right away, not allowing herself to be distracted by any beautiful or more lively tunes.

She was about halfway through the complicated piece when she heard the glass door click open. A draft blew her piano book shut. It was Jess.

"Jess! You're not supposed to be here. We'll get into all sorts of trouble again. Don't you know that?

Already the nuns are thinking about finding out where you came from so they can send you back. You better scram right now."

Jess flinched. "I came to find out if you'd figured out a plan. Have you thought of it yet?"

"Not yet." Toni smoothed her piano book open again and started to play the piece once more. The right hand alone this time.

"I was hoping you could show me how to play some more tunes. I'd love to learn how to play the piano too."

"Well, I can't tonight. I have to learn to play this dumb piece by the end of the month. Sister Celeste said that it'll be on the Royal Conservatory piano exam for sure and I don't know it at all."

"It sounded mighty good to me. If only I had my harmonica, I'd play along with you."

"What harmonica?"

"My pa gave me his harmonica for a going away present, like. That's when he got too sick and couldn't look after me anymore so he brought me to live with my auntie and uncle on their farm."

"When was that?"

"Maybe 'bout three years ago," Jess said. "And, and Uncle, he grabbed my pa's harmonica away from me and wouldn't give it back though I begged and begged."

"That's terrible! What about your aunt? Couldn't you tell her? Couldn't she get it back for you?"

"She up and died a couple months back. There was just my uncle and me on the farm now, and he's drinking something terrible since my auntie died. He's even got a still for making his own home brew whiskey under the chicken coop."

"A still for making liquor? But surely that's against the law. He could get into really big trouble for that. Maybe even sent to jail. You should really tell Mother Superior."

Jess shook her head. "I'd be too darn scared to tell her anything about him or that bloody farm. Especially after the terrible thing I did. She's sure to send me away if she finds out."

"What terrible thing you did?"

Jess flinched and shook her head. She stared at the floor and wouldn't look at Toni now. "Can't say," she mumbled. "Don't even want to think on it."

"Don't you have any other relatives who could look after you?" Toni asked her. "You must have. Everybody does. I've got tons."

"Don't rightly think I do. My uncle does have some papers of mine though," said Jess. "Important papers that my auntie told him to give me. I heard her say that just before she died. And he promised her that he would. Only I never saw them since. Maybe they'd even tell about some other relatives or something?"

"So where is this farm?"

"A ways from Bernardville. North, I think. But you won't tell anyone, will you, Toni?" Jess picked out a soft little tune on the high notes on the piano.

"No. Of course I won't tell anyone, Kiddo. Not if

you don't want me to. We'll figure out something to get your harmonica back. And those papers as well," said Toni. "But you better scram now so I can get down to business and learn this Haydn stuff."

Disgraced In The Cathedral

ON SUNDAY MORNING THE BOARDERS who had not gone home for the weekend were allowed to sleep in until 8:30. Toni was as restless as ever, but she forced herself to stay in her alcove until the wake-up bell. When it finally rang, she leaped out of bed and grabbed her uniform. She dressed carefully with a white shirt which had been freshly ironed by the kitchen nuns and her tunic, which was still a bit damp around the hem from her accident the night before. Thank goodness, her woollen stockings had dried pretty well.

She paid special attention to brushing out her hair and tying it back neatly with dark blue ribbons. *La Directrice* would be checking that their uniforms were in perfect order when they attended the Sunday High Mass at the cathedral.

All the girls lined up two by two in the corridor beside the dormitory. *La Directrice* inspected them, adjusting a tam here, straightening a tie there. Toni noticed that Jess was standing alone, shifting from one foot to another uncomfortably, forlornly. She also saw that Janeen was standing alone. Toni had noticed that her buddy Linda's alcove had been empty for the whole weekend.

Toni went to stand next to Jess. "Partner?" she asked. Jess nodded gratefully. Jess was wearing a light blue jacket a bit long in the sleeves for her. The nuns must have found it for her along with a uniform and a pair of shiny black shoes.

Toni turned to Janeen and asked, "Want to walk with us?"

Janeen's eyes widened as if she couldn't believe Toni's invitation. "Sure," she said, smiling gratefully.

In front of the line, Mother Superior reminded the girls as she probably did every Sunday, that there was to be absolutely no talking on their way to the cathedral, and certainly none whatsoever during the service. They were to occupy the front three pews beside the communion rail where they would be in full view of the whole congregation. The reputation of the convent of Saint Bernadette was very important.

"As always, the eyes of all the townspeople will be on you the whole time during Mass. Now is that understood?"

The girls all nodded solemnly. Then they followed Mother Superior down the corridor to the grand front stairway, past the big picture of Saint Bernadette, and out of the convent in two straight, solemn, and silent lines.

Toni inhaled deeply as they walked down the boardwalk at the edge of town, their feet echoing like a distant drum roll. She breathed in the pungent cool air. There was a sharp, almost delicious odour of burnt grass that somehow reminded her how hungry she was. They were not allowed to eat anything before Mass, if they were to receive Communion. They were not allowed even a drink of water, and that small supper of a half a bowl of stew the night before was a distant memory. Toni's stomach felt as empty as that high blue sky.

Yellow and brown leaves drifted down from the slim trees which lined the boardwalk. She crunched them under her feet and wished they were edible.

She was carrying her prayer book, and in her jacket pocket was her rosary purse. In with her rosary beads she had tucked a nickel which she would use to buy a candle before Mass started. She was going to say a special prayer for an idea to help Jess.

The walk to the cathedral was not long since it, as well as the convent, was at the edge of town. They had to walk past a cemetery surrounded by a tall hedge which separated the convent yard from the cathedral. The cathedral was built of the same yellow brick as the convent. It was a tall building with a high steeple topped by a gold cross which looked so high that it seemed to scratch the bottom of the sky. The bells in the steeple were ringing now, calling everyone to Sunday Mass. Toni's stomach grumbled a reply. She pulled in her stomach to stop the racket.

The boarders followed Mother Superior, marching up the broad cathedral steps to the big double doors which were held open for them by two young men with plastered down hair and wearing embroidered white blouses over long black cassocks. They looked about the same age as Toni's two older brothers. She wondered if her brothers were standing in front of the church at home, as they often did on Sundays, holding the doors open for the people there. She felt a pang of homesickness.

The strong smell of incense poured out of the cathedral. It was dim inside after the bright sun. On both sides of the large room were tall stained-glass windows with pictures of saints. The red and yellow and blue glass filtered the bright sunlight. Over a side altar was an especially beautiful stained-glass window. It was of a white bird flying with a branch of leaves in its beak and rays of golden sunlight pouring around it. The Holy Spirit, thought Toni.

As Mother Superior led the two long lines of boarders straight up the centre aisle, past all the other rows of pews, Toni studied the backs of the people already inside to see if Aunt Eloise and Uncle Ray were there, but she didn't see anyone she recognized. When they got to the front of the cathedral, each girl genuflected in turn and filed into the pews. Toni elbowed Jess so she would genuflect as well, and Janeen followed her.

Toni was glad that she was on the end beside Jess, although *La Directrice* was in the pew directly behind them. To their right was that side altar under the Holy Spirit/bird stained-glass window. There was a bank of candles where people could light a candle for a special prayer. While other people dressed in their Sunday finery quietly filed into the church, Toni turned around and pointed to the side altar, asking the nun for permission to go there. *La Directrice* nodded.

There were over a hundred candles in about ten rows on a ledge in front of the altar. They were all small and white, each in its own small glass. About half of the candles were lit. Toni dropped her nickel into a metal box at the side and, with a long stick, she lit a candle on the very top row. She knelt in front of it and stared up at the white bird with the yellow light shining around it.

She whispered her prayer. "Please dear God. Please help me. Help me think up some way to help my friend, Jess. I suppose you know all the details of her problem already. There must be some way I can help her so she won't be forced to go back and live with that terrible uncle." Toni couldn't think of anything else to say, so she just whispered, "Amen," and went back to her seat.

Four altar boys with crisp white blouses over their long black cassocks led a procession at the front of the church to stand in front of the big ornate central altar. The bishop in long crimson robes was at the end of the procession. He was splendid in his tall gold hat. There was a subdued clatter as everyone in church stood up. High Mass had begun.

The bishop sang out a greeting and the choir answered. Toni's stomach answered as well, growling loudly. She pulled it in. Beside her, she heard Jess's stomach growling as well. Then hers growled back! No matter how hard she pulled her stomach in, she couldn't stop its growling.

The singing stopped and everyone knelt down to bow their heads and pray silently. And Toni's stomach growled so loudly that she was sure everyone around her could hear it, especially since the church was very quiet now with everyone kneeling in silent prayer. Here they were in the very front of the church where the whole congregation could see them. And hear the racket of their grumbling stomachs.

Jess glanced at her through the corner of her eye and a giggle erupted from her. Toni couldn't help herself. She giggled back. She tried in vain to fish out her handkerchief to have something to smother her giggles with, but it wasn't in either jacket pocket. Not only that, but Janeen, who was kneeling on Jess's other side, started to giggle as well.

Toni's stomach growled again and more giggles burst up her throat and out of her mouth. She swallowed hard but the more she tried to stifle her giggles, the louder they became. They boiled up her throat and burst out of her mouth like a volcano. Scalding tears were filling her eyes and running down her cheeks. Beside her, Jess's shoulders were shuddering with giggles and so were Janeen's, which made Toni feel like giggling even more.

Toni felt the sudden pressure of a heavy hand on her shoulder. "Marie Antoinette Sauvé! Jessica! *Et* Janeen!" hissed *La Directrice. "Allez-vous en! Immédiatement!"* She pointed with her thumb. *"Dehors!"*

Toni glanced back. The nun's face was red with anger or shame.

Toni tugged at Jess to follow her out. She quickly genuflected and scrambled down the long aisle, not daring to look up at the townspeople who she was sure were all staring at all three of them with utter disgust. Girls giggling during Sunday Mass. Such blasphemy! She heard Janeen's and Jess's light steps behind her.

By the time they finally reached the outside door, Toni's giggles had evaporated. She pushed the heavy door open. Janeen and Jess followed her outside.

"Are we ever in trouble now!" said Toni, wiping the tears from her eyes. She looked back at the two girls.

Jess's mouth was open. Her pale eyes were huge. She looked scared. As scared as that morning when Toni had first found her in the barn.

"It's him! Oh God almighty! It's Uncle Harold! He's not dead after all! I got to get outa here!" She crouched down behind Toni's knees against the wide cathedral steps and clutched at Toni's skirt.

"What are you talking about?" asked Janeen.

Toni glimpsed a big man with a wide-brimmed hat pulled down over his eyes. He was hurrying up the walk toward the cathedral as if he was late for Mass. That must be Jess's cruel uncle! If they went down the cathedral steps, they would bump right into him. And he'd grab Jess and cart her off! There was no way they could escape from him.

Escape To The Cemetery

TONI YANKED THE HEAVY CATHEDRAL door back open. "We'll find some place to hide inside," she hissed, pushing Jess back into the dim church.

"But-but..." sputtered Janeen.

Toni couldn't stop to explain. She followed Jess back inside. Janeen shut her mouth and followed them. The entrance was dark after the bright morning.

"Come on. There must be another door." Toni dragged Jess to the side of the cathedral behind the rows of pews. Thank goodness everyone was standing now and the choir was belting forth a loud song. They could duck unnoticed behind back pews.

"Come this way," hissed Janeen, tugging at their sleeves. "There's an emergency exit over here."

Toni threw herself against the wide door and pulled Jess out after her. Janeen followed them, stumbling down some narrow steps. They ducked into some thick bushes growing against the cathedral wall. The cemetery looked a lot bigger here than on the other side of the hedge, thought Toni. There were rows and rows of headstones extending to the thick bushy hedge which surrounded the whole cemetery. No one would be able to see them there.

Jess's face was pasty white with fear. She cringed behind a moss-covered gravestone. "He-he's here! Right here! Did you see? I-I thought maybe he was dead. He's probably come into town to nab me. They musta got word out to him that I was here and he's bloody well come to get me!" She babbled on. "What can I do? He probably saw me out there in front of the church. Where can I go?" She clutched at her jacket, her thin white fingers like claws, her yellow eyes wild.

Janeen flicked back her hair and stared at Jess. "What...." she started to ask.

"Jess saw her uncle out there and she thinks he's come to get her," Toni explained as she patted Jess's arm trying to calm her. "He's a real nasty sort."

Janeen nodded, seeming to understand. "No wonder she's so scared."

"Look, Jess," Toni said. "If we went to Mother Superior and explained about how cruel he is and all his drinking and everything, maybe she won't allow him to take you away. Besides, I'm sure he didn't recognize you out there in front of the Cathedral. You look so different now even I'd have trouble recognizing you."

"But he'll say he's my bloody next-of-kin. He'll tell the nuns that and-and he'll tell them what I did and-and...." Jess was trembling with fear now. "He's right here now! Come to force me to go back to that bloody farm of his, I betcha. There's no other place I could go."

"That sure doesn't sound fair, Jess," said Janeen. "Don't you have any other relatives who could take you in?"

Jess took a deep jagged breath and shook her head. "I don't remember any. When we were living in the city it was just my pa. And he got really sick. And before that, my mom and my little sister. But they got that terrible influenza and died. That was years ago. There was no one else."

"But what happened to your pa?" asked Janeen. "Where is he now?"

Jess shook her head sadly. "We ain't never heard of him since that day he brought me to live with my auntie on the farm."

"What about those papers you told me about last night?" said Toni. "You know. Those important papers from your father?"

Jess crossed her arms tight to stop trembling and gnawed on her bottom lip. She took a deep breath and calmed down a little. "Right. There must be something about money in those papers. I do remember Auntie saying that when I was old enough, they'd use the money my pa left with them to send me away to a school somewhere so I could learn music proper like. I do remember her saying that. Oh, Toni. If I could only get those papers from him. Maybe there's even something in them about some other relative who'd take me in until I was all growed up."

"That's it, Jess! We'll just have to go out there to his farm and grab back those papers. The farm's not that far away, is it?"

Jess shook her head. "We couldn't, Toni. I know we bloody well couldn't. It took me days crossing over the fields to get way over here to the convent. And, and I bloody well know if I went back there he'd just up and grab me and, and I'd never get away. Ever."

"You have to do it, Jess. You have to get those papers. They rightfully belong to you. I'll go with you and I won't let him do anything to you. I just won't allow it."

Jess bit her lip again and shook her head. "There's something I haven't told you, Toni." She glanced up at Janeen, then back down at her hands.

"It's all right, Jess," said Janeen. "I wouldn't ever tell anyone."

"Well, um," Jess started slowly. "That last day on the farm, I-I did something awful. Something just terrible. I um...." She swallowed hard and licked her lips. "He'd grabbed away my pa's harmonica, see, and he wouldn't give it back. And he was beating me all over for spilling some chicken feed and he just wouldn't stop."

Janeen shook her head. "He sounds like a monster!"

"He is," said Jess. "But anyways, I up and grabbed this broken bottle and threw it hard, straight in his face. It caught him on the forehead, and then there was blood spurting out from his head like an underground spring. And blood was all over the place, his face, and dripping down between his fingers. Oh, it was so darn terrible! He screamed bloody murder. Then he keeled over into the muck and lied there so still, I thought he was dead! I thought I'd bloody well killed him. Me, killed the man! So I just picked myself up and scooted off as quick as I could."

"Where did you go?" asked Janeen.

"First I scrambled under some brambles in a ditch out in the back field and hid 'til nightfall. Then I high-tailed out of there. Oh, you see, don't you? If I went back to his farm he'd come after me with that pitchfork of his and he'd run me through with them prongs. I know he would. So you see, I got to leave. I got to high-tail outa here right now before he gets to them nuns and tells them the whole story and about him being my rightful uncle and then drags me back to that farm of his and lets me have it good and proper. That'd just be the end of me." Her voice ended in a high pitched squeak.

"But Jess. Jess. If you do run away now, where would you go?" said Toni. "You'd starve before the week's even over. That's if you don't freeze to death first."

"But if I went now, at least I'd have a chance."

"I agree with Toni," said Janeen. "You can't just

run off. Not now with winter coming."

Toni held onto Jess's arm to stop her from taking off. "What can we do?" she asked Janeen.

"I don't know, but I'm sure we'll think of something."

Toni didn't know either exactly how they could help Jess, but she did know for sure they couldn't let her just run off.

The organ music from the church flowed out into the cemetery. They were singing the Gloria now. That meant High Mass was almost over. They'd have to think of something fast, or else it was true: Jess's cruel uncle would probably come and grab Jess away. Her stomach bunched into a knot and grumbled loudly again.

"I'm so hungry I can't think straight," she muttered, holding her stomach.

Jess nodded. "So I better just get going right now before they start coming outa church. That Mass business must be almost over."

Toni tightened her hold on Jess's arm and looked up at the sky. Grey clouds were billowing about on the horizon. They seemed to be drifting toward the town. The wind had picked up and, although the sun was still shining brightly, the wind had a cold bite to it.

"You can't go now, Jess. Think. Where would you go? Hide out in someone's barn again? You don't have any food, and that thin jacket won't keep you warm through even one night. Look. How about coming back to the convent for dinner? Sunday dinners here must be the best. I bet they'll even have chocolate cake for dessert."

"Hey, remember it's your turn to be the server at our table?" said Janeen. "You can't leave now, Jess. You just can't."

Jess looked about to cry. She blinked fast and shook her head and rubbed her hands together. "Chocolate cake?" she croaked.

Toni nodded. "I'm sure I smelled chocolate cake being baked last night. Right, Janeen?"

"Right."

"Look, we'll all feel a lot better once we've had some dinner. Then I'm sure we'll think of something."

Jess kept shaking her head. Her pale eyes were huge with fear. "But he's so big and he'll be so blasted mad and...."

"He won't hurt you, Kiddo," Toni said, raising her chin and pushing back her shoulders to look as tall and strong as she could. "I promise. I won't let him even touch you. I won't let one single thing happen to you. If he does show up at the convent, I won't let him take you away."

"You really promise?"

"I really promise," said Toni. "Cross my heart and hope to die. I promise that I'll stick to you like glue every single minute. That uncle of yours won't be dragging you away anywhere, Jess. I'll yell and scream. I could even call up my mother on the telephone. Or my aunt. They both used to be very important students here at the convent."

Janeen nodded. "Sounds like a good plan."

Jess's nose was running. She sniffed loudly and wiped it on the back of her jacket sleeve.

Toni fished around in her tunic pocket for her hanky. There it was. She shook it out and handed it to Jess. "Pretty clean," she said.

"Thanks, Toni. You sure this is the best way?"

Toni nodded her head slowly. "There's no other way I can think of right now. We'll have to face the music. But I'll be right with you the whole time. You'll see."

"Come on," said Janeen. "I know where there's a hole in the hedge so we can take a shortcut back to the convent."

"And that chocolate cake," said Toni.

Jess nodded and said, "You're a darn good friend. You know that Toni? And you too, Janeen."

When Toni saw Janeen smile at Jess, she tried to remember why she called her, what was it? 'Mean Janeen'? With that smile she didn't look one bit mean. She crossed her arms over her stomach and forced herself to grin bravely at Jess as well. "Aw, it's nothing, Kiddo," she said, giving her shoulders a quick hug. As long as the kid didn't know how scared she really was.

As the cathedral Angeles bell rang out, ending the Mass and announcing the noon hour, she pulled Jess up from behind the gravestone and they both followed Janeen, picking their way between the graves to the bushy hedge on the other side of the cemetery.

Toni wished there was another way. The thought of confronting that tall, powerful-looking farmer, even if he was only half as mean as Jess had told her, scared Toni all the way down to her toes. But she couldn't think of any other way, so they'd have to do it. They would have to face the music. But they would face it together.

Facing The Music

"HERE'S WHERE WE CAN SQUEEZE through the hedge," pointed Janeen.

Toni nodded and gently pushed Jess forward. She crawled reluctantly into the dense prickly hedge. Toni was right behind her. As the three girls emerged into the convent yard, picking twigs and leaves out of their hair, Toni saw the other boarders were just returning from Mass.

At the end of the line marched *La Directrice*. She spotted Toni, Janeen, and Jess and her eyes blazed.

They brushed off their tunics. Toni took a deep breath and stood straight beside Janeen, ready to face the nun's anger. Toni thanked her lucky stars that at least Mother Superior wasn't there. She could feel Jess cowering behind her shoulder.

"Les voilà, les trois renégates!" The nun went on speaking in such fast angry French at them that

Toni didn't know what she was saying, although by her tone and her sharp red nose, she certainly got the general idea.

"Excusez-moi, ma Soeur," she interrupted after a few minutes. *"Je ne comprends pas."*

Janeen stepped forward. *"Les filles. Elles ne vous comprennent pas,"* she told the nun that Toni and Jess didn't understand what she was saying.

The nun waved her hands about and said something to Janeen. Then Janeen turned to Toni again and said, "She's saying we really let her down in church today. That the whole town will think the convent is full of disrespectful girls."

Before Toni could answer, *La Directrice* said slowly and deliberately, so Toni understood every word. *"Après le diner, nous parlerons encore. Avec la Mère Supérieure. Et avec votre tante aussi."*

"Oui, ma Soeur," Toni gulped and stammered, bowing her head. Oh no! They were going to call her aunt! Was she ever going to be angry!

The nun looked at Janeen and shook her head. Then she turned and stalked away into the convent

Most of the girls remained outside to soak up the warmth from the weak sun. Some of them stood around Janeen, Toni, and Jess, interested in what was happening.

"Boy! Is she ever mad!" Janeen said, flicking back her dark hair and looking at Toni with both eyes.

"I guess we deserve it," said Toni. "Thanks for helping us out. I really had no idea what she was saying."

Jess nodded.

"What did you do, anyway?" asked Betty, the taller of the dark-haired sisters who sat at their table.

"Well, um, it's kind of embarrassing, but our stomachs were grumbling like crazy and we started to giggle during Mass and couldn't stop," said Toni.

Janeen grinned. "That happened once last year to me and Linda. For penance we had to wash windows for a whole week, so we'd better brace ourselves. Maybe they'll make us do it for two weeks."

"Where's Linda gone?" asked Toni. "I saw that her alcove's been empty since Friday night."

"She's gone home again for the whole weekend, lucky duck. Her dad came to pick her up on Friday after supper."

"Don't you ever get to go home for the weekend?" asked Toni.

"Na. My mother's way too busy doing her dancing all the time. She has to travel all across the country performing, so I never get to go home. This year I'll probably even have to stay here during Christmas holidays like I almost did last year."

"Christmas holidays in the convent? That would be so dismal." Toni shook her head.

Janeen nodded and flicked back her hair again. "If it wasn't for Linda inviting me to her house for Christmas, I'd have been the only girl here. Must admit I sure was mad that day when the nuns moved me away from the alcove across from Linda's."

"And gave the alcove to me? So that's why you were so mad."

"That's those nuns for you. You just get a good friend and they'll try their hardest to keep you apart."

"So why can't you go to Linda's for Christmas holidays this year?"

"Her mom's real sick now, so Linda's not sure if I'll be allowed to."

Toni shook her head. No wonder Janeen didn't like anyone to come between her and her best friend. "So your mother's a professional dancer?" she said. "What's her name?"

"Josephine Lavolé. You heard of her?"

"Really? Josephine Lavolé? That's your mother? Wow! My mom took me to see her perform when she came to Vancouver last year. My mom said she's the most famous student Saint Bernadette's has ever had. In fact, after seeing her I decided that I wanted to be a dancer for sure when I grow up. I thought she was so wonderful."

"Yeah," Janeen screwed up her face as if she had something nasty in her mouth. "Maybe."

Before Toni could figure out what she meant by that, the bell for dinner finally rang.

TONI WAS RIGHT. There was chocolate cake for dessert with dinner. So far nothing else had been said about their shameful giggling in church. Toni almost expected that they might miss out on the dessert for penance, but there was a piece of cake for her, one for Janeen, and one for Jess as well. The way *La Directrice* was looking at her, Toni was sure she would have plenty to say to them after dinner, but she tried not to think about it.

She was finishing the last delicious cake crumb when she noticed Mother Superior swishing into the Refectory. She bowed to *La Directrice* and whispered something to her. *La Directrice* bowed back and beckoned to Jess to follow Mother Superior.

Jess grabbed Toni's arm. "Oh no! He must be here to get me!" she hissed. "What should I do now?"

Toni had already decided that there was no way she'd allow Jess go anywhere alone. "We'll both go," she whispered back, trying to look brave.

Jess shoved the rest of her cake into her mouth and as Toni led her out of the Refectory, Janeen smiled at them sympathetically. "Good luck!" she whispered after them.

Mother Superior was waiting in the hallway beside the Refectory door. "It is not necessary for you to come as well, Marie Antoinette. I called for just Jessica. This is a private family matter."

"But I won't go without Toni, um, Marie Antoinette," cried Jess. "I just won't! She said she'd stay with me every single minute. She promised!"

"Jessica wants me to come along, Mother Superior," said Toni. "She asked me to, specially."

Mother Superior sighed heavily. Then she said, "Very well then. You may both follow me. We are going up to my office. Someone is waiting there to see you, Jessica."

Jess gulped. Toni nodded to her and tried to smile confidently. Although she was feeling far from confident.

They followed Mother Superior up the two flights of stairs and down the corridor to her office. The nun walked briskly, silently, her head erect. It was all Toni and Jess could do to keep up with her. Toni knew Jess was scared, but this was something they had to do. She felt as if they were both doomed prisoners on their way to the executioner.

When they got to Mother Superior's office, the nun paused with her hand on the brass doorknob. She glanced back at the girls.

"Marie Antoinette. It is not necessary that you come into my office. As I said, this is a private family matter. You may wait out here in the corridor."

Toni raised her chin. She looked defiantly into Mother Superior's dark eyes behind their glasses. There was no way that Mother Superior was going to make her wait out here. She had promised Jess that she was going to stick to her like glue and that's exactly what she intended to do.

"No, Mother Superior," she said. "I promised Jess that I would stay with her the whole time."

Mother Superior looked at her for a minute, then she sighed again. "Very well, Marie Antoinette," she said. She noticed that Jess's chin was blotched with chocolate icing. She fished into one of the pockets in her voluminous skirt and pulled out a large white handkerchief. She gently wiped Jess's chocolatey chin with it. Then she straightened her braids and patted her hair. When she looked satisfied with Jess's appearance, she opened the office door and ushered the girls inside.

Jess hung back, shaking her head at Toni. By now, Toni's lips were frozen into an encouraging smile. She linked arms with Jess and pulled her into the office.

The first thing Toni noticed about the farmer was his smell. The stench and stuffiness of Mother Superior's usually pristine room met them like a solid wall. There was a nasty mixture of smells from the farmer's filthy boots, his unwashed clothes, and his stinky alcohol breath. Although he was sitting on a straight-backed chair beside Mother Superior's desk, Toni could see that he was a huge man. With his heavy woollen trousers and large overcoat he seemed to overflow the chair. His coat was unbuttoned to reveal a shirt, once white, with stains down the front which the shiny black tie didn't cover.

He was sitting with his right boot, encrusted with farm dirt, crossed on his left knee, his thick fingers tapping impatiently on Mother Superior's desk. His face was reddish, newly shaven. A long jagged scab slashed across his high forehead.

Must be from that broken bottle Jess said she had thrown at him, thought Toni. He looked older than Toni had thought he was from her brief glimpse in front of the cathedral. But he was at least as big and strong as she remembered.

Toni took a deep breath, lowered her head and

pushed forward. She drew Jess along to stand directly in front of the farmer.

"Ah ha!" he said. "So here's the prodigal at last." His gravelly voice was thick with drink.

Jess cringed away and if Toni hadn't been holding onto her arm firmly, she would have escaped out the door then and there. But Toni gripped her arm more firmly and pulled her even closer.

"So!" the farmer blared down at them. "So this here's where the chick's been hiding out. Well I came to get you on home, girl. Home's where you belong."

Jess shook her head. Toni could feel her trembling beside her. "No," Jess told him in her gritty voice. "I'm not going anywhere with you."

"What!" he bellowed " 'Course you bloody well are, girl. You got to."

"Well, I'm not," said Jess. "I'm bloody well staying right here in this here convent."

He shook his head, his faded blue eyes bulging with anger. If Mother Superior had not been right there, Toni was sure that he would have grabbed Jess then and there and carted her off.

Mother Superior cleared her throat and said, "I am sure you have some proof that this child should be allowed in your custody, Mr. Jenkins?"

"I sure do, Ma'am." He opened his overcoat and fished something out from his inside pocket. A large brown envelope with "For Jessica" written on it with black letters and a shiny harmonica. He slapped them down on Mother Superior's desk.

"My harmonica!" Jess squealed and pounced on the instrument. She snatched it up and clutched it close. "And that envelope's mine too! That's the envelope my pa left for me!" She tried to snatch it from under his hand as well but he held it fast.

"You're darn right it's from your pa, girl. You can have that devil's instrument back. But it don't matter what you say, you bloody well got to come home to the farm with me. That's what your pa said right here in his will." He jabbed the envelope with a thick finger.

"His will? But we don't know for sure if Pa's even dead."

"Ain't he? Well, he may just as well be dead. We ain't heard from him for years. Not since that day he brought you to the farm. So, come on, girl. Let's get going on home."

"No! No, I'm never going back to that awful place. Not now. Not never!"

"Told you, you got to. It all be right here." With shaking hands the farmer pulled out a document from the envelope. "The last will and testament of Harvey Sweeney," He screwed up his eyes and read. "Dated April 10, 1931. To whom it may concern. All to be held in trust for my daughter, Jessica Louise Sweeney, until she reaches the age of eighteen, by my only living relative, my cousin, Matilda Jenkins."

"But anyways, that's Auntie, not you, and she, she ain't here no more."

"As her husband, the right passes on to me. So

you see, you got to come back to the farm. I need someone to do for me. The whole place is going to the dogs. In fact the bank's threatenin' they'll not renew my loan if I can't clean it all up. Right now the house looks like a regular pig sty and I ain't had me a decent cooked meal since...."

Toni felt her face flush as her anger and her courage grew. She could no longer hold her tongue.

"And you expect Jess to go back to your stinking farm and slave for you? Well she won't. No siree. Not after the way you treated her, she won't. I, for one, won't let her."

The farmer snorted through his nose at Toni and laughed in her face. "A spirited young scalawag we bloody well got here."

Toni turned to Mother Superior who was watching all this silently.

"Oh, Mother Superior!" she pleaded. "You can't let him take Jess away. All those bruises and cuts, they're mostly from him beating her. She told me. They weren't from falling off any horse, like she said. They don't even have a horse on that farm. That's what she told me. That man is a regular monster."

"Now look here, Sister," said the farmer. "I might bash the child around a bit now and then. But only when she needs it. I'm a true believer in 'Spare the rod and spoil the child.' As I'm sure you are too."

Mother Superior looked down at Jess. Jess wouldn't look at her now. She hung her head and stared at the floor. Toni knew how embarrassed she was about those lies she had told Mother Superior.

"You got to tell her, Jess. You got to tell her the whole truth. Now!"

The room was silent except for the ticking of that pendulum clock. Finally Jess raised her pale eyes to Mother Superior and swallowed hard. She nodded. "It's all true what Toni, um, I mean, what Marie Antoinette said. I didn't really fall off a horse. I got most all these here bruises and cuts from him. Or tryin' to get away from him."

"Oh, she's a fine one to talk," the farmer growled. "She's one nasty little piece of baggage, that one is. You musta seen it here already, Sister. Lyin' and stealin'. And violent! See this here cut." He pointed to the jagged cut on his forehead. "Well, she done that to me with a broken bottle. Threw it right in me face, she did. Then left me lyin' there in the stinkin' muck. Coulda darn well of been dead."

"But I-I had to. He kept beatin' me and beatin' me. I had to run away from...."

"And that's not the last beatin' you'll bloody well be getting from me, girlie," he roared.

Toni squared her shoulders and stepped between Jess and the raging farmer. "What about that still you have under your chicken coop, Mr. Jenkins?" she said, loudly and clearly, staring him straight in the eye. "Jess told me all about that still where you make liquor all the time."

"What! She told you about that!" The wound on the farmer's forehead seemed to pulse with fury.

"How dare she!" He shoved Toni aside and reached out with huge red fists to grab Jess. "Just wait till I get my hands on you, girlie, I'll...."

Jess squealed and cringed away from his grasp, ducking behind Toni's shoulder.

"Mr. Jenkins!" Mother Superior's stern voice cut off the farmer's tirade. "This child will not be going anywhere with you. Now. Or ever. I would never allow any child in my care go off with such a brute as you appear to be. Now, if you would be so kind as to give us those documents, we shall see if we are able to get to the bottom of Jessica's family and plan properly for her future."

The nun stood tall in front of the farmer, her dark eyes flashing fire.

The farmer flinched from the nun's attack. "Humph!" he huffed. "Humph!" he huffed again. "But that girl. She's my wife's niece. Her next-of-kin. You got no rights to keep her here, Ma'am. No rights at all," he blustered.

"As you well know, Mr. Jenkins, I have been in touch with the proper authorities. The police, as a matter of fact. And you may get in touch with them as well, to complain if you wish. I am sure they would visit you at your farm promptly. Perhaps they would even investigate a certain, um, production under your chicken coop, which Marie Antoinette has just mentioned? Meanwhile this child shall remain here at the convent where I know she shall be safe."

"Chicken coop?" his voice squeaked. His eyes

flashed at Jess, then at Toni, but they both straightened their backs and stared right back at him.

The farmer opened his mouth and closed it again. He seemed to be fishing around for words, but none would come. He couldn't even look at Mother Superior now. Finally he threw the envelope onto her desk and stumbled out of the office, his back bent. Defeated.

"Wow!" thought Toni, staring admiringly at Mother Superior. "Wow! Now that's power!"

"Oh, thank you, Ma'am," said Jess. "Thanks loads for saving me."

"My goodness!" said Mother Superior, brushing off her skirt. "What a bluster! That man is certainly a tyrant! I must admit that for a moment I wasn't sure what to do. I think we both should thank Marie Antoinette for mentioning that, um, illegal production under his chicken coop."

"But what will happen to Jess now?" asked Toni. "Where will she go? Could she stay here?"

"Certainly. There will always be a place for her here at the convent."

"Oh, that's so great! Ain't that so great, Toni?" squealed Jess, grabbing Toni's arm. "I get to stay here for ever and ever."

But then Mother Superior crossed her arms and raised her eyebrows. "Now, another matter, girls," she said. "I understand from *La Directrice* that you two and Janeen Lavolé were behaving most inappropriately at High Mass in the cathedral this morning."

Toni bowed her head and stared at the floor. Just when she was hoping that Mother Superior had forgotten about them giggling in the cathedral. "Sorry, Mother Superior," she mumbled. She looked up into the nun's dark eyes behind their glasses. "We didn't mean it, but we both got the giggles so bad. We just couldn't help ourselves. The harder we tried to stop laughing, the worse it got," she tried to explain.

"I'm real sorry too, Ma'am," said Jess. "I promise you that I won't never, never laugh again for my whole entire life."

"Oh, you mustn't promise such a thing, Jessica." Toni could tell that a smile was twitching at the nun's lips. "But do you girls know the penance for being so disrespectful in church?"

Toni nodded. "I heard it was washing windows."

"Right," said the nun. "For one week. You shall begin tomorrow. And don't let such behaviour happen again."

"Washing windows is better than mending any day," said Toni.

"And lots better'n muckin' out an old stinky pig sty," said Jess.

At that, Mother Superior had to laugh right out loud. She hugged both girls at once, one under each arm.

The Renegade Dancers

A FEW WEEKENDS LATER WAS THANKSgiving, and when Aunt Eloise invited Toni to come over for the long weekend, Toni asked if she could bring along two friends as well.

"Two friends? You've made two friends already? Certainly. It would be lovely to have them."

Mother Superior said that a change of scene would probably do them all some good, so she agreed to allow Jess and Janeen to go along.

The first night after everyone in Aunt Eloise's farm house had settled, the three girls crept downstairs in their nightgowns and bare feet and snuck out the back door. It silently whooshed shut behind them, and they whisked down the back steps.

It had stopped raining completely, and a bright moon sailed through wispy clouds. Toni saw that Jess's smile lit up her whole face. The moonlight glinted on her harmonica as she held it high over her head in triumph.

"I got it!" she shouted. "I bloody well got it back! Yippee!"

"Hush, now," said Janeen. "You'll wake up everyone." But she was grinning at her.

Toni grabbed Jess's hand, and they swooped across the damp backyard to the barbed wire fence. Janeen dashed behind them. They all squeezed under the fence and bolted out into the tussocky fields. Then they raced down the rows of wheat stubble until they were all breathless. They stopped in the middle of a great field which stretched out on all sides to the very edge of the huge star-studded black velvet sky.

All was silent around them except for their panting and the wind. The perpetual prairie wind.

Then away in the distance, they heard it. The honking grew louder and louder until they could see the V of flying geese, the moonlight touching their outstretched wings with silver.

"The geese. They must be heading south for the winter," said Toni.

"South, where it's always warm and sunny," said Janeen, breathing hard.

Jess blew into her harmonica, a long answering call to the geese, wishing them well on their journey to a better place. Then she found the tune, the dancing tune, the prairie dancing tune. She played it and the music soared up to the gliding birds.

Toni grabbed Janeen's hands and, whirling around

Jess, they danced in the moonlit stubble of the fields. Toni and Janeen danced to Jess's prairie music over the fields under the velvet sky. They danced and danced, and Jess played and played until they were all exhausted and spent. Then they all dashed back to the warmth and safety of Aunt Eloise's house.

About the Author

NORMA CHARLES sold over 100,000 copies of her very first children's book *See You Later, Alligator.* Since then, she has published five juvenile novels, including *No Place For A Horse, April Fool Heroes* and 1998's *Dolphin Alert!* Several of her books have been translated into French and published in Québec. In addition to her books for children, her short story "Lum King" received a best-short-story award in Coquitlam, British Columbia.

Born in small-town Manitoba, Norma Charles grew up there and in British Columbia. She attended a year of high school at Gravelbourg, Saskatchewan's College Mathieu, which is the basis for the convent in *Runaway.* Norma worked in the British Columbia school system for many years as a teacher and librarian, retiring in 1995 to write full time.